W9-BHR-627

VENGEANCE

ANNE SCHRAFF

SADDLEBACK
EDUCATIONAL PUBLISHING

SADDLEBACK
EDUCATIONAL PUBLISHING
www.sdlback.com

© 2012 by Saddleback Educational Publishing
All rights reserved. No part of this book may be reproduced in any form or by any means, electronic or mechanical, including photocopying, recording, scanning, or by any information storage and retrieval system, without the written permission of the publisher. SADDLEBACK EDUCATIONAL PUBLISHING and any associated logos are trademarks and/or registered trademarks of Saddleback Educational Publishing.

ISBN-13: 978-1-61651-961-2
ISBN-10: 1-61651-961-4
eBook: 978-1-61651-961-2

Printed in Guangzhou, China
0512/CA21200822

16 15 14 13 12   1 2 3 4 5

CHAPTER ONE

The United States was well established as a world power in the early twentieth century. It was then that President Franklin Roosevelt won the Nobel Peace Prize for negotiating peace between Russia and Japan in 1905." Mr. Jesse Davila, senior history teacher at Cesar Chavez High School, was lecturing.

The class broke out into snickers and, in a few cases, outright laughter.

Ernesto Sandoval, senior class president, winced as Rod Garcia broke out into loud guffaws. Then Garcia declared loudly enough for the teacher to hear, "Dementia strikes again." Rod's friend, Clay Aguirre, chuckled loudly.

1

Mr. Davila looked mortified. "Did I say *Franklin* Roosevelt? I'm sorry, I meant Theodore Roosevelt, of course." Poor Mr. Davila, Ernesto thought. He was a good teacher, but he was dealing with problems at home. Misspeaking was no big deal to Ernesto, but some students in the class were clearly out to get the teacher. The class continued without Mr. Davila making another gaffe.

However, the teacher wasn't himself lately. Somebody had told Ernesto that Mr. Davila's wife had Parkinson's disease. Also, his daughter and her child, a freshman at Chavez, were living with them. Caring for the grandchild, Angel Roma, was largely in the hands of Mr. Davila. Ernesto thought the poor man had good reason to be distracted sometimes. Ernesto couldn't understand why the kids couldn't cut Mr. Davila some slack. Why couldn't they show some compassion for his troubles?

After class, a little knot of students continued to discuss Mr. Davila. Rod and

Clay led the discussion. They were saying that the teacher was obviously too old to be at Chavez High and that he should retire. Ernesto, his girlfriend, and his best friend got near the group. They could hear what was being said.

"He's gotta be in his middle sixties," Rod Garcia declared. "That's *old*." Rod had run for senior class president, and Ernesto had beaten him. Ever since then, Rod hated Ernesto. Rod felt the office was his because he had headed so many boring clubs during his first three years at Chavez. Then, last year, Ernesto Sandoval, an outsider from Los Angeles, joined the student body as a junior and walked off with the position. Rod considered Ernesto a thief who took what was rightfully his.

"Yeah," Clay Aguirre agreed. "The old guy isn't fit to teach anymore. He should be fired. We deserve better."

Naomi Martinez, Ernesto's girlfriend, chimed in. "That's so unfair, you guys. Mr. Davila is an excellent teacher. This is

3

my favorite class this year. Anybody can make a mistake."

Clay Aguirre glared at Naomi. She was probably the most beautiful senior at Chavez, and she had dated Clay for a long time. But Clay had treated Naomi rudely, and one day he went too far. He slapped her in the face, leaving a bad bruise. That was the end of their relationship. Soon after that, she and Ernesto started dating. Clay hated Ernesto for that. Clay and Rod were united in their hatred of Ernesto Sandoval. They both felt he had taken something precious from them.

Abel Ruiz, Ernesto's best friend, was the first guy to befriend Ernesto when he came on campus last year. Abel spoke up. "You guys are nuts. Mr. Davila's a sharp guy. He's made American foreign policy clearer to me than any teacher ever."

"But he *is* awfully old," a girl piped up. "He's the age of my grandfather!"

"So what?" Ernesto said. "Any of you know how old Benjamin Franklin was when he helped draft the Declaration of Independence? He was seventy. And when he took part in the Constitutional Convention, he was eighty-one. I wrote a paper on him when I was a freshman. I was blown away by what this guy did in his old age."

"You're such a know-it-all, Sandoval," Rod griped bitterly.

Naomi grinned at Ernesto and winked.

Ernesto, Abel, and Naomi walked on toward the vending machine before going to their next classes.

"Sometimes I think there are people with no hearts at all," Naomi commented. She pondered the peaches and pears in the machine's little windows. "Can't they have a little pity for a good man like Mr. Davila who makes a little slip? We *all* make mistakes, but they pounce on him like wolves."

She slipped coins into the slot, chose the peach, and spoke again. "I'm so ashamed of the fact that I actually used to date Clay! What was I thinking? What a mush head I was. And he'd make me write papers

5

for him and get mad when I wasn't quick enough."

Abel got an orange drink, and Ernesto got a box of raisins.

"You know what really bothers me?" Ernesto remarked. "All that rotten stuff that those jerks text and tweet about Mr. Davila, it's gonna get back to the administration. Mrs. Sanchez sitting there in the principal's office, she's gotta know about it. I love my iPhone and Facebook, but all that can be a weapon against somebody you're out to get. In five seconds, you can ruin a reputation."

Abel Ruiz used to be an average student without any big dreams in life. Then Ernesto encouraged him to develop his talent for cooking. Now Abel was making fabulous dinners for his friends and worked as a junior chef at the Sting Ray, a ritzy seafood restaurant. He planned to go to culinary school after graduating from Chavez.

When Ernesto started a program at Chavez where seniors paired up with at-risk freshmen, Abel was the first to sign up.

Abel's freshman little brother was Bobby Padilla. Bobby was a kid who'd run away from home and was a handful for his single mother.

"How's it going with Bobby?" Ernesto asked as he popped raisins into his mouth.

"Pretty good," Abel replied. "He's a nice kid. I think I'm enjoyin' it as much as him. Y'know, all my life I lived in the shadow of my big brother. Oh yeah, my brilliant, wonderful big brother, Tomás. But now, at last, I'm the big brother to a little guy who actually looks up to me. I'm tellin' you, dude, it's a trip." Abel took a slug his orange drink.

"I like my little freshman girl too, Angel Roma," Naomi added.

"Is she an angel?" Ernesto asked wryly.

"Not really," Naomi admitted. "But then neither am I. She has some problems at home. You know her mom's Mr. Davila's daughter, and there are problems there. But she seems to relate to me. Your idea for this senior-freshman deal is really good, Ernie.

7

Like so many kids drop out of Chavez in the tenth grade. If we can keep them interested through that time, maybe they'd make it to graduation."

Later that day, Ernesto, Naomi, Abel, and his on-and-off girlfriend, Bianca Marquez were sitting together at lunchtime. They were eating what they had brought from home. Eating at the cafeteria was getting too expensive.

"Look!" Bianca announced. "Abel made my lunch today!"

"Wow," Ernesto remarked.

"Yeah, he made me these ham and cheese *tortilla* roll-ups," Bianca explained. "Abel kept the filling in his little cooler, and it's all fresh. I shouldn't be eating so much, but it looks so good." Although she was too thin, she thought she was overweight.

"I've got a crummy cheese sandwich with really ugly yellow mustard," Naomi complained. "I think the bread is kinda stale too. Ernie, I may have to drop you as a boyfriend and steal Abel from Bianca."

"You guys," Abel said, "I got enough stuff for two more *tortilla* roll-ups. Dump your sandwiches in the trash."

"He's a saint!" Naomi declared.

"Absolutely," Ernesto agreed.

Within a minute or so, they each had a freshly made *tortilla* roll-up.

"Know what?" Bianca said. "I got four text messages about a Mr. Davila. I don't have him in class. Do you guys know him?"

"Yes," Ernesto replied. "We have him in United States as a World Power."

"You poor things!" Bianca said, rolling her eyes. "All those text messages say he's an awful teacher. He's so senile he doesn't know what he's saying."

"That's a lie!" Ernesto objected. "You're getting those text messages from some creeps who're out to make Mr. Davila look bad. He's a good teacher."

"What have they got against the poor guy anyway?" Abel asked. "I'll never understand people. I mean, he hasn't hurt anybody. He's a fair grader. He's easier

9

than most teachers. Why do they just wanna hurt some poor guy who's trying to get by like the rest of us? Sometimes I think I'd like to go out in the desert and live with the animals. Even if a mountain lion got me, you know, it'd be just because he's hungry. I can understand that. But people—why just hurt other folks for no reason?"

"I guess," Ernesto suggested, "it makes some jerks feel good to be putting down somebody else. I'm gonna text my friends about what a good teacher Mr. Davila is."

"Good idea," Naomi agreed. "I'll do it too. Fight fire with fire."

"What makes me really sick," Ernesto remarked, "is that this creepy stuff is gonna get back to Mr. Davila. My homie, Julio Avila, he told me he heard Mr. Davila's wife has Parkinson's disease. They got a lot to deal with at home."

"What if you'd tell those creeps the kind of problems he has?" Bianca suggested. "Maybe they'd cut him a break."

Ernesto laughed. He didn't want to be cynical, but asking for mercy from Rod and Clay was just not realistic. "The weird thing is," Ernesto responded, "those guys, Clay and Rod, they come from pretty well-off families. They get everything they need and want. You could understand if they came from some down-and-out family or were getting abused or something. But, no, they got it made in the shade."

Naomi had finished her *tortilla* roll-up and started speaking. "Thanks, Abel. That was fabulous." She thought about her own family, which was not really ideal. Felix Martinez, her dad, had an explosive temper. He used to bully Naomi's mother and brothers. At one point, the brothers had gotten so sick of his bullying, they ran away. Luckily, the family members were reunited, thanks to Naomi and Ernesto.

At the end of the week, the principal of Cesar Chavez High, Julie Sanchez, slipped into the back row of Mr. Davila's class. Ernesto's heart sank. The slander had reached her. She wanted to see for herself how much of it was true. Mr. Davila looked terribly nervous when he saw her. Ernesto glanced over at Naomi, and her eyes were filled with pity too. She shook her head.

But Rod Garcia and Clay Aguirre looked triumphant. They grinned at one another as if to say "Mission accomplished!" Like bloodthirsty dogs, they had treed their raccoon, and Mrs. Sanchez was here for the kill. Ernesto was not a violent person. But at that moment, he dreamed of catching Rod and Clay in some dark alley and knocking them both on their backs. He wouldn't do it, of course, but he enjoyed the thought.

Ernesto suddenly recalled that Mr. Davila looked his best when a lively discussion was going on in class. Ernesto had an idea.

"We . . . uh . . . dealt with President Roosevelt's extension of American power beyond our borders last time," Mr. Davila began.

Ernesto's hand shot up.

"Yes, Ernesto?" Mr. Davila asked, looking grateful that someone had a question. He was especially pleased that Ernesto Sandoval was posing the question. Mr. Davila sensed that the boy was on his side.

"President Roosevelt really signaled aggressive American foreign policy, didn't he?" Ernesto began. "He was somebody who wasn't afraid even of going to war to advance national interests."

"Yes, indeed," Mr. Davila agreed, noticing then that Naomi's hand was up. She had taken her cue from Ernesto. She was now thinking what he was thinking: A lively class discussion would make Mr. Davila look good. They could show Mrs. Sanchez that their teacher inspired his students to get into his subject with enthusiasm. "Yes, Naomi," Mr. Davila said.

"I remember this one quote from President Theodore Roosevelt that you put in our study guide, Mr. Davila," Naomi continued. "It really made it clear to me where he was coming from. 'No triumph of peace is quite so great as the supreme triumphs of war.' I mean, I don't think President Roosevelt was a warmonger or anything like that. But he was willing to risk losing the peace if the cause was important enough."

A boy in the middle of the room raised his hand. Mr. Davila nodded toward him. "I think Roosevelt would be called a hawk today," the boy stated. "You know, how back in the days of the Vietnam War, they had hawks and doves. Well, Theodore Roosevelt wasn't any dove."

A smattering of chuckles showed general agreement with that sentiment.

"Do you think President Roosevelt actually sought war?" Mr. Davila asked. His own nervousness was fading as he got caught up in the excitement of the discussion.

"No," Abel Ruiz answered. "I think he talked big and tough to scare wannabe enemies. He didn't act as . . . um . . . as belligerent as he talked. I think the whole deal was to scare everybody into thinking

14

he was a big, bad dude. Then maybe they wouldn't have to have a war."

"Very good, Abel!" Mr. Davila responded.

Hands were going up all over the classrooms. More students wanted to express either their admiration for President Roosevelt or their disagreement with his blustering ways.

The class that day was one of the best Ernesto could remember with Mr. Davila. Ernesto stole a quick look at Mrs. Sanchez in the back of the room. She looked interested and engaged. Rod Garcia and Clay Aguirre looked frustrated.

Mr. Davila did not misspeak except at the very end. He called the Panama Canal the Panama Railroad, but the slip went by so fast that Mrs. Sanchez didn't even seem to hear it. At the end of the period, Mrs. Sanchez stood up and announced, "Thank you, Mr. Davila. And thank you, wonderful seniors. I enjoyed the class, and I'm delighted by how involved you students are in the learning process."

As the students filed from the room, Rod Garcia approached Ernesto. "You're really something, Sandoval," he snarled bitterly. "You and your cronies maneuvered the class to make it look like the old dude was doing great. I gotta admit, Sandoval, you're good. You're really good. You can pull stuff off that I hardly believe."

"What have you got against that teacher, man?" Ernesto demanded.

"I deserve the best education I can get, dude," Rod snapped. "No demented old man has the right to deprive me of that. My father's the CEO of a company with fifty employees. He has to cut some loose all the time if they're dead weight. He says it's like pruning a bush. You don't get rid of the dead stuff, the bush doesn't thrive. A bleeding heart sap like you would keep all of them around until they drove the company into the ground. I'm not done here. I'm gonna make sure the principal finds out what's really going on in this class."

After school, Ernesto went down to the used car lot. It was where he had bought his first car, the Volvo he still drove. He had mixed feelings about the big white Volvo. It was maddeningly reliable, costing him very little in repairs. It was a safe car. That was something his parents and Naomi reminded him of almost every day. Once Naomi had seen a photo of a horrible automobile accident. A little sports car had been reduced to rubble. She showed the photo to Ernesto to remind him of what a car looked like if it didn't have enough protection.

But Ernesto was embarrassed to be driving the old Volvo. Some time ago, he'd pulled into a parking lot and parked. Some nice old retired man came over, smiled, and looked at the Volvo. Then he congratulated Ernesto for having such good sense. It was good too see him, the man said, in a safe, reliable car instead of in one of those "hot rods some of these punks are driving."

Ernesto had smiled cordially, but he didn't appreciate the compliment. It was like a seventeen-year-old girl being praised for wearing her grandmother's clothes.

Even Ernesto's friends wondered why he was still driving the Volvo. Abel Ruiz had a VW Jetta. Naomi had a gold classic American car. Carmen Ibarra had a jelly red convertible. Her boyfriend, Paul Morales, who was Ernesto's good friend, just recently bought an electric blue Jaguar. The Jaguar was very old—much older than Paul—but it was a *Jaguar*, man!

Sitting in his sturdy, reliable Volvo, Ernesto felt totally outclassed. He had to do something about the car. Yet, as he drove it onto the used car lot, he felt like a betrayer. He kind of felt as though the Volvo had become a friend. And his friend was now grief stricken. How could Ernest abandon someone who had served him so faithfully?

The used car dealer came smiling to Ernesto's window. He was rubbing his hands together eagerly. He was not the same man who had sold Ernesto the Volvo. He liked that other guy better.

"Ah!" the man declared. "You're getting tired of driving your grandma's car, eh, boy?"

Ernesto swallowed hard and got out of the Volvo. He glanced at the shiny Hondas, Toyotas, Dodges, Fords, all vying for his attention. He made the mistake of glancing back at the Volvo. There it stood, waiting patiently like an old white horse. Even in the dusk, Ernesto thought he saw moisture in the headlights. Ernesto could not rid himself of a silly and impossible thought: Oh man! It's crying!"

Ernesto Sandoval left the used car lot without trading in his Volvo. He assured himself that he would do it soon, but not right now.

CHAPTER TWO

During dinner at the Sandoval house that evening, Ernesto mentioned Mr. Davila and what was going on.

Luis Sandoval, Ernesto's father, also taught history at Cesar Chavez High. He knew all the other members of the department. "I know Jesse well. He's a nice man," Dad remarked. "And he knows his stuff too."

"Rod Garcia and Clay Aguirre are leading the pack, spreading rumors," Ernesto said, swallowing a bite of dinner. "They're sayin' that Mr. Davila has dementia or something just because he misspeaks once in a while."

"That's nonsense!" Ernesto's father snapped. "He's a sharp guy. When we talk about history, I'm amazed at the breadth of his knowledge."

Mom got a hard look on her face, and she spoke. "Rod and Clay should be ashamed of themselves for acting like that. Don't their parents teach them anything about common decency?"

"The sad part of it is," Luis Sandoval responded, "you can't deal with stuff like that in a way that wouldn't embarrass Jesse. He's a great guy. He served in Vietnam. He's a hero. We sometimes talk about our war experiences, mine in Iraq and his in Vietnam. He went through much more than I did. Those guys who served in Vietnam went through a terrible time. Then, when they got back home, they didn't even get any thanks. Now his wife has Parkinson's disease too, which is awfully hard on her and the family."

"What's Parkinson's disease?" Katalina asked.

"It's a chemical problem in the brain, sweetheart," Dad explained. "The arms and legs shake, and there's a kind of stiff walk. Jesse told me his wife has had this for almost ten years, but it's worse now. Her speech has been affected. Tension can make the symptoms worse. So if any of this nastiness against Jesse gets back to her, it's only going to make the poor woman worse."

A dark look came to Katalina's face. "I hate those boys who're being mean to Mr. Davila," she declared.

"No, *mi hija*," Luis Sandoval commanded gently. "Never use the word 'hate.' Don't scar your heart and soul with that word. You are against what they are doing, but you do not hate them."

Juanita looked at Ernesto and asked, "Can't you tell those boys to stop being mean to Mr. Davila? Can't you tell them how sick his wife is and they gotta stop?"

Ernesto took a deep breath. He didn't say so out loud, but he felt as Katalina did. At the moment, he hated Rod and Clay. "It wouldn't do any good, Juanita.

They don't care about other people. They just care about themselves, and they think Mr. Davila isn't a good teacher."

"Another thing too," Luis Sandoval added. "The Davilas have their daughter and her little girl living with them too. She's a single mother, and her child is fourteen, a freshman at Chavez. Imagine how the poor kid is going to feel if this garbage about her grandfather gets back to her?"

"Dad," Ernesto responded, "you know this project we got at Chavez this year? You know, where the seniors adopt some at-risk freshman? Well, Naomi Martinez has taken Mr. Davila's granddaughter, Angel Roma, as her little sister. She's getting along good with her."

"That's wonderful, Ernie," Dad declared. "The little girl is lucky to have a senior big sister like Naomi. That girl has a big heart. I've said it before, Ernie, but I'm saying it again. You have introduced so many good programs into the senior class. I'm very proud of you, son."

"It's not just me, Dad," Ernesto protested. "Deprise Wilson, our senior activities advisor, she's been right there with me through all this. It means so much that I've got an ally like that. And my homies, they're behind me too. If it was just me, it would all go over like a lead balloon."

"There you go with that word again, Ernie," Maria Sandoval remarked. "Your 'homies.' Oh well. Anyway, Naomi is a beautiful soul, and that's for sure. I can't get over the fact that she's Felix Martinez's daughter. He can be such a strange, angry man, and those brothers too—big, tough, wild creatures. I'm sure they're good boys at heart. But when I see the whole Martinez clan together, all of them yelling, rough-housing, braying like mules. It's a little frightening."

Mom shook her head. "Do you remember, Ernie, when the youngest one, Zack, was trying to drive his truck when he was drunk? You tried to stop him, and you got all bloodied up. I was just so shocked that they'd attack you . . . "

Ernesto smiled a little. "Mom, *they* didn't attack me. It was one of Zack's friends."

"Yes, well," Mom admitted, still shaking her head. "I remember you hanging over the sink with the blood dripping . . . "

After dinner, Ernesto called Naomi. She had taken Angel Roma for a frozen yogurt after school.

"How'd it go with Angel, babe?" he asked.

"Good," Naomi reported. "We had strawberry yogurts. She's kinda shy, but she talked a little bit. She told me how nice her grandfather is to her. She's really upset with her grandma's condition, though. She told me her grandfather was going to retire from teaching this year, but he can't now because of medical bills and all. Angel is a sweet kid, but she's got a lotta anger too. It's stressful around the house, and something else is going on too. I'm not sure yet what."

Ernesto wondered what "something else" was going on but didn't ask. Instead, he spoke about the history class that day. "I think Mrs. Sanchez got a good impression of Mr. Davila's class today. I hope that takes the pressure off the poor guy. He doesn't need any more problems."

Then Ernesto remembered why he called in the first place. "Oh, by the way, babe, I'm gonna be looking for a new used car this weekend. Want to come along and help me pick something out?"

"Oh? You're getting rid of Viola?" Naomi asked.

"What?" Ernesto asked. "Who's Viola?"

"Your Volvo of course," Naomi replied. "She's such a sweet car, so trustworthy. I feel so good when you're in that nice safe car. You're a great driver, Ernie, but some other people aren't always that good. If somebody hits you, being in Viola will protect you better than most cars."

"Naomi, when did my creepy-looking Volvo with the dented back fenders become Viola?" Ernesto demanded.

"Oh, I thought you knew, Ernie. Hasn't she *always* been Viola?" Naomi answered.

Ernesto had never thought of the Volvo as a female car. That was just going to make parting with her—it—all the harder.

"No," he insisted, "it's just a banged-up old Volvo that's outlived its usefulness. I want something hot. I want a car I can be proud of. Have you seen Paul Morales tooling around town in that electric blue Jaguar?"

"Yeah, but that's Paul," Naomi countered. "He's sort of the outlaw type."

"Oh yeah? Well, what am I? The wimp type?" Ernesto asked. "All my homies drive Jags and Jettas, and I'm stuck with . . . with Viola. Well, I got news for you, babe. Viola goes this weekend."

"She's so old," Naomi remarked. "I suppose they'll send her to the crusher. Turn her into scrap metal."

"What?" Ernesto asked. He hadn't thought of that.

"She won't find a new home. Nobody'll want her," Naomi said, playing on Ernesto's feelings.

"Knock it off, babe," Ernesto said, a little ruffled. "We're not talking about the family pet. We're not talking about a dog. We're talking about a rusty old car whose time has come."

"I suppose you're right, Ernie," Naomi sighed. "When you're old, nobody wants you. That's life, I guess. Like poor Mr. Davila. He's over the hill, and the vultures are descending. It'll happen to us someday too. We're young, Ernie, and we think it'll always be that way for us. But one day we'll be like Viola and Mr. Davila, heading for the scrap heap."

Ernesto knew he was being played. He sighed deeply. "Naomi, Mr. Davila is a human being!" he groaned.

"It's just a metaphor, Ernie," Naomi replied.

He changed the subject, they chatted a little, and then they ended the call.

Much later, Ernesto stayed up late working on a project for AP American History. Mr. Bustos was very demanding, and Ernesto was determined to get those college credits. It was almost eleven o'clock when his father poked his head through the bedroom doorway.

"Ernie, I just got a text from Hortencia," Dad reported. "She was closing up when she saw a lot of police cars heading in the direction of the high school." Hortencia Sandoval was Dad's younger sister. She operated a restaurant and tamale shop, which was only a block from Cesar Chavez High School. "I'm going over there now, Ernie."

"I'll come too, Dad," Ernesto responded.

"You sure?" Luis Sandoval asked. "It's pretty late."

"Yeah," Ernesto said, following his father to the family's minivan. They drove the short distance to the street just before the high school and walked the rest of the way. They noticed a lot of police action at the school.

Luis Sandoval recognized a police officer who was a close friend of his lawyer brother, Arturo. "Hi, Jerry!" Ernesto's father called to him. "What's going down?"

The police officer recognized Luis Sandoval as one of the teachers at the school. "Some vandalism," he answered. "Somebody got in the library and spray painted everywhere."

"Oh man!" Luis Sandoval groaned. "Just what we need. The school budget's so tight we can hardly afford needed improvements."

"Does it look like gangs did it?" Ernesto asked.

The officer looked at Ernesto. His own son was a senior at Cesar Chavez High School. The boy must have told his father about the great new senior class president, Ernesto Sandoval. "Hey . . . you must be Ernie," the officer replied. "My son talks about you all the time. No, it doesn't look like gangs. They're not into that kinda thing. Likely some kid got ticked off by a bad grade from a teacher or something. It looked like some kind of rage."

Julie Sanchez, the principal, came walking over to the Sandovals. "Isn't this awful?" she asked, frowning. "I got in touch with maintenance. They'll be working for the rest of the night to repaint as soon as the police give us the okay. Luis, I know that sounds like overreacting. But there's some very rough language on the walls."

"Good," Ernesto's father said, nodding. "I wonder how the kid got in?"

"Doesn't it just break your heart that one of our students would do something like this?" Mrs. Sanchez fretted. "Some kid so mad about something. Won't even try to talk to someone. Just goes ahead and vandalizes the school."

"I'm glad they didn't damage the mural," Ernesto remarked. The mural had special meaning for Ernesto and most of the students. Two of Ernesto's friends, Dom Reynosa and Carlos Negrete, had been dropouts and taggers last year. Then Ernesto, Abel, and Luis Sandoval convinced them to return to school. They painted the beautiful mural of Cesar Chavez and his friends on the side of the school. Even in the darkness, Ernesto could see the power and the beauty in the faces of Chavez, Robert Kennedy, and Chavez's tireless colleague, Dolores Huerta. Many of the weary but determined farmworkers they championed were painted there too.

"Thank God nobody touched that," Mrs. Sanchez said. "That's such a great asset to our school."

When students arrived at Chavez High in the morning, all evidence of the vandalism had been erased. Still, everyone seemed to know what had happened. Students who lived nearby and their friends had been tweeting one another overnight.

As Ernesto walked onto the campus, Rod Garcia shouted, "Did ya hear about the school being vandalized last night, Sandoval? Dirty language all over the library walls?"

Ernesto didn't answer Garcia. He just shrugged his shoulders. The less he had to do with Rod Garcia, the better. But that only inflamed Garcia. He came closer and started taunting. "Don't want to talk about it, eh? I don't blame you, Sandoval. You don't want to own how much our lousy school spirit is making kids so angry. So much for your leadership of the senior class. Got to have been a senior to do something that bold, or maybe a couple of them."

Ernesto just wanted Garcia to go away. He kept walking, but Rod just kept going. "Maybe they're sick of your antics, Sandoval. Lotta kids frustrated by how you're running things, man. Last year we had a lotta spirit. The football games were packed. Nobody's building up spirit for our teams anymore. At the senior class meetings, all we hear about is another stupid goody-two-shoes scheme of yours. You're setting up ridiculous programs for the freshmen instead of taking care of the seniors."

Ernesto stopped short and wheeled around to face Garcia. Rod took a half step back. The look on Ernesto's face was a little scary. "Rod," Ernesto snapped angrily, "some pathetic loser came in the library and spray painted the walls. Maybe it wasn't even a student. It's got nothing to do with me or anybody else."

"Yeah?" Rod persisted. "Funny, we didn't have any vandalism last year. You're not making the seniors proud of the school. That's what the senior class is supposed to do. Make everybody proud. The sports rallies are like wet dishrags. You don't care about sports, dude, but sports—especially football—that's the heart of a high school."

Ernesto felt like telling Rod Garcia what he really thought of him and his theories. But he knew better than to do that. He had to keep his cool. He was senior class president. If he sank to Garcia's level of abuse, he would be discrediting his office and the school. "The police are investigating, and they'll find out who did it," Ernesto said as he walked away. Garcia didn't follow him. He'd finally given up.

A few minutes later, Naomi caught up to Ernesto. "It's so sad," she remarked. "I got five text messages last night about vandalism."

"Thanks to the wonders of Twitter and iPhones, news spreads fast," Ernesto responded flatly. "When did the first ones start coming in?"

"Around eleven," Naomi said. "They were from our friends, Carmen, Tessie . . . some other kids."

"I guess it's easy to be mad at the school if you get a lousy grade or something," Ernesto suggested. "But it's a cowardly way to show your anger."

"A lot of the parents really demand good grades from their kids," Naomi replied. "And let's face it, some kids do their best, and they just can't measure up. They're between a rock and a hard place. One girl I don't know very well, she called me. She said she was happy about what happened.

35

She said maybe school would be cancelled for a couple days. She just wanted more time to study for her science test. She said if she gets one more C minus, her parents are confiscating her laptop."

Ernesto shook his head. "I don't know," he objected. "I don't see someone taking such a chance and doing something like this just to buy time. Whoever did this was really furious about something else, something a lot more serious. I mean, there are a lot of kids going here whose parents don't put much pressure on them. I think whoever did this was venting their rage at . . . life. The school's a handy target. A lotta kids are sad or mad. They don't see any light at the end of the tunnel."

"I guess," Naomi agreed sadly.

"You know, Naomi," Ernesto said bitterly, changing the subject, "that dude Rod Garcia is still at it. He's been yelling at me already this morning. Got me as I walked on campus. He's sure a senior did the vandalism, and he's got it all figured out. It's my fault for not whipping up enough spirit for the football team. Garcia thinks if we just had more kids yelling for the Chavez Cougars when they make a touchdown, everything would be okay."

"What a creep," Naomi responded.

"Yeah," Ernesto affirmed. "He's still mad about me passing out pictures of that kid who was missing—Bobby Padilla. I spent like four minutes at the senior class meeting alerting kids about a fourteen-year-old freshman who'd been missing for a week. All I asked is maybe everybody could keep their eyes open. Man, that inflamed somebody to go spray paint the library? That's what Garcia thinks."

"You'd think he'd be ashamed," Naomi remarked. "You guys found Bobby, and now he's back in school doing fine. And Abel Ruiz is really putting his heart into this big brother thing, and he's doing Bobby a lot of good. I think Bobby's doing Abel some good too. Abel's been so used to being the loser in his family. Now, suddenly, there's a younger kid looking up to him. So it's win-win."

"Rod once called me a megalomaniac who thinks he can save the world," Ernesto responded. "That's why I get involved with kids like Bobby. Naomi, I don't think I can save the world. Nobody can do that alone. I just want to help somebody who comes across my path when I can do something."

The boy and girl walked for a second or two in silence. Then Ernesto spoke. "It's like a story I heard once. This dude was on the beach picking up starfish that'd washed up on the sand. He was tossing them back into the ocean so they wouldn't die on the beach. Somebody came along and told him he was a fool 'cause he couldn't save all the starfish on the beach. But the dude just said, 'I can save a few, and that counts for something.'"

Ernesto was quiet, reflecting. Then he went on. "I'm not a big shot, Naomi. I mess up the same as everybody else. But

I can put in some programs that help our kids here, like seniors mentoring seniors and the big brother, big sister program. I mean, why not? Even if we save one kid's future—even it it's just one—then maybe it's worth it."

"Babe," Naomi said, slipping her hand into Ernesto's. "Did I ever tell you I am proud of you?"

Ernesto smiled. Naomi turned toward him and buried her face briefly in his chest, "I love you, Ernie," she whispered. "I love you like crazy."

"Love you back, babe," Ernesto responded. He put his hand on her back and ran his fingers through her long, silky hair.

CHAPTER THREE

After school on Wednesday, Naomi Martinez walked over to the freshman area of the Chavez campus. The yogurt shop across the street was having a special on frozen mango and peach yogurt, two for the price of one. Naomi's little sister, Angel Roma, had enjoyed it so much before, Naomi was springing for another trip.

"Hi, Angel," Naomi called out cheerily when she saw the girl.

Angel broke from the girls she was with and hurried toward Naomi. "Hi, Naomi," she replied. Usually she took the school bus to her home on Finch Street. But today Naomi was taking her home in her car. Naomi had gotten her mother's permission the day before. On the short walk to the yogurt shop, Angel remarked, "You're so fun, Naomi. I'm so glad you're my big sister!"

"I'm glad to have a little sister like you, Angel," Naomi responded. "You know, I have three brothers and no sisters at all. I always wanted a sister, but instead I got three big jerky brothers. But I love them. Still, now I got my sister, too."

Angel was an attractive fourteen-year-old, but she wasn't beautiful. She had pretty dark eyes and long lashes. Though only fourteen, she was already almost as tall as Naomi. She had been put on the at-risk list at Chavez because of some truancy and rebellious behavior. So she was someone at risk of dropping out of school.

The girls ordered their yogurts and sat down at a table.

"You know, Naomi," Angel commented as she took a spoonful of her yogurt. "My grandma's sick. She has this Parkinson's disease, and it's so awful. I mean, I love my grandma, but I hate it when I have to take her for walks like every day after school. She kinda shuffles along real weird like, and she holds on to me. The doctor says exercise is real important for Grandma, so she needs to walk every day. Mom works, and Grandpa doesn't get home till late, so I'm stuck with it. The only reason I could be with you today is 'cause Grandpa said he'd get home as soon as he could."

"Well, that's a big responsibility for you, Angel," Naomi agreed.

"Some kids in my class come on our street," Angel continued, "and they snicker and say mean things. I'm so embarrassed. They go, 'There goes Angel and her zombie grandma. Maybe Angel's a zombie too.' They're so mean, Naomi. They make fun of me at school too. They ask me if I'm gonna get Parkinson's disease pretty soon too. And then they say I'll for sure be a zombie like Grandma. I hate those girls so much. Sometimes they walk behind me at school trying to imitate how Grandma walks. The other kids laugh and laugh and . . . " Angel poked hard at the yogurt, her eyes suddenly filling with tears.

"Kids can be so awful sometimes," Naomi remarked. She was shocked at what she was hearing, but she kept her voice calm. "I'm really sorry that's happening to you, Angel."

"Naomi, I wish I didn't have to go to school at all," Angel confessed.

"You have to, Angel," Naomi insisted. "You need the education so you can graduate and get a good job and have a nice future." Naomi had lost her appetite for the mango peach yogurt, even though it was delicious. She picked at it, taking only tiny bites.

The girl was silent for a few moments, and then she spoke. "If I tell you something really, *really* evil, Naomi, will you hate me forever? Will you stop being my big sister?"

Naomi turned numb. "Of course not, Angel," she answered.

"Sometimes I wish Grandma wouldn't be there anymore," Angel confided. Her dark eyes had grown even larger and darker. "That she'd die or something." After the girl said it, she looked frightened. "I must be a terrible, awful person to think stuff like that, huh, Naomi?"

"Maybe this is the 'something else going on' that I suspected," Naomi thought without saying so out loud. Then she spoke carefully to her little sister.

"No, Angel, you don't really mean it. It's a big burden for a young girl like you to be taking care of someone that disabled. In your heart, you don't want your grandma to die. You just want that burden to go away. You're scared. We sometimes have awful thoughts rushing through our minds. How we feel is not our fault."

"Did you *ever* in your whole life have such a bad ugly thought, Naomi? I bet you never did. You're so sweet and nice." Tears ran down Angel's cheeks. "You *never* had an evil idea . . . "

"Ah yes, Angel, I did," Naomi told the girl. "I had job once where I was really scared. I worked at a frozen yogurt shop, and I loved working there. But an old man owned the restaurant, and I was so terrified of him. When he stayed away for a long time, I was hoping he had died. He was very old, and I would have been happy if I never had to deal with him again. Looking back, I realized that I didn't really want him to be dead. I was just so glad to be rid of the problem."

"Did he die?" Angel asked, her eyes wider than ever. Naomi could understand her tears and her guilt. Angel was thinking that her bad thoughts about her grandmother might actually cause her to die and that her death would be Angel's fault.

"No," Naomi answered. "But he went away to a hospital, and I never saw him again."

The girls finished their yogurts in silence. Then, as they walked from the shop, Angel commented, "Grandma has this funny way of talking too. It's like slurred or something. Some girl from my class heard it. Now when she sees me at school, she imitates Grandma, just to make fun of me."

"Angel," Naomi asked, "do you have any nice girls in your class who are friends with you? When I was your age, a freshman at Chavez, there were mean girls too. But I had this little group of friends who stuck by me. They helped me make it through. It was us against the world. We need friends so much. It's hard to face the world alone."

"I have one friend," Angel responded. "She's really, really nice. She stands up for me. Sometimes she yells at the mean girls and threatens them. I like her a lot. Her name is Penelope."

Naomi only knew one Penelope in the freshman class. "Penelope Ruiz?" she asked. That had to be Abel Ruiz's little sister.

"Yeah," Angel said, brightening. "Do you know her?"

"Yeah," Naomi replied. "Well, I know her big brother, Abel, real well. He's one of my best friends. He's my boyfriend's *very* best friend, and we all like Penelope."

"Sometimes Penelope's brother picks her up at school," Angel remarked. "But Penny said they fight a lot."

"Yeah," Naomi said. "Brothers and sisters fight sometimes, but deep down they love each other. Abel would do anything to help Penny if she needed it."

"Naomi, I never told anybody how much I hate walking with Grandma," Angel admitted as they reached the car.

"Well, I'm glad you shared your story with me, Angel," Naomi assured the girl. "When something is bothering you, it helps to tell somebody else instead of keeping it all bottled up inside. When you just keep it inside, it's like putting a lid on a kettle of boiling water. If you don't take the lid off, it kinda explodes."

Angel looked sorrowful as she got in the car. "It's not Grandma's fault that she's sick like that. Grandma is only sixty-three years old, she sighed. "I mean, that's old and stuff, but not really, *really* old. Most people aren't sick like that when they're sixty-three. Grandma gets real depressed sometimes, and that makes me feel worse."

"Angel, just try to be nice to your grandma," Naomi advised. "Don't pay any attention to those mean girls. They're bullies. When you ignore bullies, sometimes they stop bothering you. It's more fun for bullies to taunt somebody they can hurt. You just hang with Penelope. And you and I'll plan some fun things, Angel. We'll go to the Safari Park some weekend. Would you like that?"

"Yeah!" Angel cried.

Naomi drove over to Finch Street. As the girls arrived at the door, Mr. Jesse Davila opened it.

"Hi, Grandpa!" Angel greeted. "This is Naomi Martinez, my new big sister."

Mr. Davila smiled at Naomi. "I know this young lady, Angel. She's one of the best students in my class," he responded.

Angel gave Naomi a hug and hurried inside the house. Mr. Davila remained at the door for a moment. "Naomi," he said sincerely to her, "it's a really lovely thing you're doing. It means so much to my granddaughter. Ernesto Sandoval is a splendid young man to have come up with this program for children under stress."

Naomi thanked the man but didn't know what else to say. After a moment, he smiled, went inside, and closed the door behind him.

Before going home, Naomi texted Abel Ruiz: "My little sister really likes Penelope. Angel says Penny is her best friend."

As Naomi was pulling into her own driveway on Bluebird Street, her phone rang. It was Abel.

"Hey, Naomi, I'm glad the kid has a friend," he said. "Guess what? My magnificent brother, Tomás, is coming to visit for the weekend. Mom's ecstatic. It's like the King of the Universe is coming. I think I'll hang out with Bobby Padilla."

"Well," Naomi advised, "*try* to be nice."

"I'll do my best," Abel replied.

At lunch at Cesar Chavez High the next day, to asked Abel how it was going with little brother Bobby Padilla.

"Great," Abel responded. "I really like the kid. We kinda click. I never got along with Tomás, and Penelope and I fight a lot. But you know, you guys? Penelope said somethin' last night that made me feel sorry for the kid. Penny said she was havin' a hard time making friends at Chavez, and so far she had just one friend." Abel turned to Naomi, "Angel Roma, the girl you took on as a big sister."

Naomi turned to the other kids in the group and explained. "Angel and I had frozen yogurt yesterday, and she said she really liked Penelope."

They all went back to munching their lunches for a few seconds.

"Heard anything more about the vandalism?" Ernesto asked after a while. "I've seen some stupid tweets but nothing solid."

"The police are investigating," Naomi remarked. "But I don't think it's priority number one. I mean, they have a lot of serious crimes to deal with. Spray painting dirty words in a high school library is probably on the back burner."

"Yeah," Abel agreed. "Some nut probably just blowing steam about something. There's plenty goin' on in school to be angry about."

Abel took a small bite of his sandwich, chewed, and swallowed. He had more to say. "I was hanging with Paul and his brother, David, last night. David said the closest thing to being in prison is to be stuck in school with the bullies and the freaks that you can't get away from. I mean, some guy whacks you, waddya you gonna do? Complain to the teachers? That gets you in worse trouble. I tell Coach Muñoz that some dude put a lotta hurt on me. Coach is gonna give me a look that says, 'Hey, you're almost a man, dude. Handle it.' Now down at the Sting Ray if the nutty busboy decks me with a frying pan, I call the cops. But in school, how come we're supposed to take the abuse? I don't get it."

"It's not only boys, Abel," Naomi commented sadly. "Angel Roma is really getting harassed by some mean girls. They taunt her when she goes walking with her disabled grandma. The poor kid is really stressed out."

"Oh yeah," Abel added. "She told Penny about that. One time, Penny even saw it going on. These two losers were stumbling down the street, pretending they were zombies. They were imitating Angel and her grandmother. Penny went after them with a huge palm frond. You know, the ones that fall off the Washington palms. They took off running."

When Abel Ruiz got home that night, his mother was frantically cleaning the house for her elder son's visit.

"Gosh, Mom," Abel remarked, "you think Tomás'll have a stroke if there's dust on toppa the doors?"

"Don't be sarcastic, Abel," Mrs. Ruiz commanded. "I want my son to come home to a nice, clean house. He's very particular. When he was living at home, his room was always so clean and neat." Mom smirked at Abel. "Unlike yours, which looks like a tornado has struck."

Penelope was lounging in a leather chair in the living room. "Mom, you know that boy at school I said I liked, but he didn't like me?" she asked. "Well, does he *ever* not like me. I walked up to him today and asked him if he'd like to eat lunch with me. He just goes, 'You're so fat, you should be skipping lunch, girl.' He actually said that. I was just totally sick, Mom. *Am I really that fat?*"

"No, you're not, Penny," Mom assured her, but in a scolding voice. "But you *do* eat too much candy. It wouldn't hurt you to skip the candy bars for a while. Did you know Tomás won't even touch candy? When he's hungry, he eats a carrot stick." Mrs. Ruiz carefully dusted the top of the piano.

"I'm sick to death of hearing about him, Mom," Penelope snarled.

Abel glanced at his sister and whispered in a voice that Penelope could hear but not their mother. "You and me both, kid."

"I don't understand you and your brother, Penelope," Mom declared. "I would think you'd be so proud of your older brother. He's just been awarded the honor of being the top student in the sophomore class at college. He said they gave him this marvelous parchment in a walnut frame. We should all be proud of him."

"You know what, Mom," Abel suggested. "I think the U.S. Constitution should be amended to let us have a king. Then Tomás could be king."

Abel and Penelope's father, Sal Ruiz, heard the comment and laughed. He worked at menial jobs landscaping for his wife's cousin. He had just entered the room, grimy and not smelling very good.

"For heaven's sake," Mrs. Ruiz cried, "will you change your clothes and shower,

Sal? Tomás will be here in less than two hours." When Mr. Ruiz disappeared down the hall to clean up, Mom shook her head. "It's nothing less than a miracle that a boy like Tomás came from this family with a father like that," she lamented.

A little later, when Penelope and Abel were alone in the living room, Penelope made a confession. She rarely confided in Abel but she told him, "I hate school. Angel Roma and I both hate it. The mean girls make fun of Angel because of her grandmother. And they make fun of me 'cause I'm fat. I wish I never had to go to school again."

"You're not fat, Penny," Abel told her. "I bet that creep who said you were fat really likes you, and he hates to admit it. Guys sometimes treat chicks bad 'cause they like 'em. Especially guys that age. Hey, school's a creepy place for most of us."

"Yeah, I don't blame whoever it was who sprayed the library walls," Penelope said.

"My little brother, Bobby, he said he thinks he knows who did it," Abel stated.

"Who?" Penelope gasped.

"I'm not telling you, Penny," Abel replied. "You'd text it to everybody, and maybe it's not even true. Anyway, Bobby thinks it was a freshman who's in trouble with his history teacher, Mr. Lucas. Lucas is supposed to be tough, and this dude is always bein' sent to the principal."

"Yeah, I've got Lucas," Penelope remarked. "He's an ogre. The boys in that room are really bad. They talk all the time when Mr. Lucas is talking. They're mean too. That punk who said I was fat—Rocky Salcedo—maybe he did it. Yeah, he'd do something like that." Deep bitterness filled Penelope's voice. "I'd love to see him busted for something."

Penelope turned pensive. "You know, there was a real nice older guy who liked me a while back. We met on Facebook. His name was Max Costa. He even gave me a ride to school. But then he just disappeared."

Abel focused intently on his laptop. He didn't want his facial expression to betray what happened to Max Costa. Abel knew all about the guy. Abel had found out that some older guy was hitting on his little sister. He and his friends tracked him down and scared him off. Paul Morales and Cruz Lopez learned that the guy was nineteen, even though he said he was only sixteen. Abel thought a grown man had no right to be hitting on a fourteen-year-old girl, especially if the girl was *his* sister.

Abel would never forget the night he, Paul, and Cruz cornered Max and threatened him. Paul Morales showed his switchblade, just to scare him. Max Costa almost passed out.

Penelope never found out what really happened to the guy.

"I guess Max was just fooling me when he said he liked me," Penelope now said wistfully. "I guess I *am* fat and ugly. No boy'll ever want to be with me."

"Come on!" Abel chided. "You shouldn't be meeting guys on Facebook anyway. He was probably a lot older than he said he was. That's dangerous, Penny. You don't wanna be doing that. You're lucky he had second thoughts about what he was doing and cut out."

"I wish I didn't have to be in school at all," Penelope complained. "Me and Angel feel the exact same way. It's just a big drag. And pretty soon that creep is gonna be coming through the door, and Mom is gonna go nuts—"

Mrs. Ruiz appeared, her face red with anger. "Did you just call your brother, Tomás, a creep, young lady?" she demanded.

"Well, *he is*," Penelope shrieked. "All he ever does is brag, brag, brag. When he starts describing all the wonderful stuff that happens to him, I could puke!"

"Penelope Ruiz!" Mom cried. "I am ashamed of you!" Mom's voice was wavy and emotional. "It is just so hurtful for a girl to talk about her brother that way."

58

"Well, it's the truth," Penelope declared defiantly. "He makes me want to puke!"

Abel leaped up from the laptop. He had a brainstorm. "Know what, Mom? Why don't I take Penny over to the mall to buy those jeans she's been wantin'? You and Dad can welcome Tomás and have some quiet time together. Me and Penny'll be back for dinner."

Mrs. Ruiz had been shocked and hurt by Penelope's hostility to her other son. Abel's proposal came as a welcome relief. "Yes, Abel, thank you," she replied. "That's a very good idea. Maybe your sister will have a chance to get over her ridiculous, child-ish spell of jealousy. Maybe she'll be more willing to welcome her brother appropri-ately. Then we can all have a nice family dinner with Tomás."

CHAPTER FOUR

Come on," Abel urged, heading Penelope out the door toward his Jetta.

Penny followed him, but she was still cranky over her mother's scolding.

"I haven't saved enough money yet for the jeans," Penelope wailed.

"I'll cover the difference," Abel promised, grabbing Penelope's arm and propelling her down the driveway. "My own dating life is in the pits. So I'm saving lotsa money from my wages at the Sting Ray."

Tears ran down Penelope's face as she climbed into the Jetta. "I don't know what got into me, Abel," she cried. "I don't hate Tomás. But . . . my life is falling apart. I flunked a math test today. And I'm in trouble in history. And that rotten Rocky said I was fat. And everybody's bein' mean to me at school. And—oh Abel, do you now what some girls did to me last week?"

"No, what?" Abel responded as he backed from the driveway.

"There's a picture in the gym of our volleyball team, and I'm in the picture making a play," she explained. "They cut out a picture of a pig and pasted it over my face. I about died!"

"Oh man," Abel groaned. "Well, shopping'll make you feel better."

"I shouldn't even be buying jeans, a fat thing like me," Penelope wailed.

Abel sighed. "You're not fat. Just try some on. You'll be surprised how hot you look."

Abel couldn't believe what he was saying. He'd never gotten along well with Penelope since they were much, much younger. They stopped being good friends when Abel turned ten and she turned seven. Before then, she was a cute, sweet little girl, but then she got a temper and an attitude. Now they mostly fought.

But Abel always loved Penelope. Deep down, Abel loved his sister very much. That's why he enlisted the help of his homies to drive Max Costa away. He was a threat to Penelope.

But now, in some strange way, Abel and Penelope were allies. They were the underdogs in the family. They stood in the blinding radiance of Tomás Ruiz, fair-haired child, prince of all he surveyed.

The rest of the ride was quiet. Abel was pondering his new relationship with Penelope. And Penelope was getting over her tantrum.

"Ohhh!" Penelope cried. "Look at these jeans. Ohhh! This is just what I've been looking for, straight leg denims. Oh, they look so good. That horrible Candy Tellez wears these. I hate her so much. She wears like a size zero."

For Abel, nowhere on earth was worse than the girls jeans department. Perhaps being a salt mine in Siberia was worse, but he didn't think so. At the moment, he was ready to try it. But Abel had no choice. He had to take Penelope out of the growing argument between her and their mother. If war had still been raging when The Great Tomás returned, Mom would've died of embarrassment.

"They come in sizes four through twelve," Penelope announced.

"What size do you usually get?" Abel asked. He glanced around, noticing that he was the only male in the department. He felt like an idiot. He wished he could put a shopping bag over his head.

"I been able to squeeze into a six. But the last time I got a six, Mom said I looked like a sausage," Penelope groaned.

"So take a six and an eight, maybe a ten, and go in there and try 'em on." Abel motioned toward the fitting room. Several mothers with their teenaged daughters stared at him. Abel felt his face grow warm. Two more teenaged girls looked at Abel and started giggling. Maybe they were sophomores or juniors at Chavez. That thought horrified Abel.

One of the girls, the bolder of the pair, approached Abel. "You work at the Sting Ray, don't you?" she asked.

"Uh yeah," Abel sputtered.

"I'm Cassie Ursillo's sister," the girl told him.

"Oh," Abel responded. Cassie worked at the Sting Ray too. She was related to Pedro, Abel's boss as the Sting Ray. She and Abel got off to a bumpy start, but now they got along.

The two teenaged girls giggled again. Cassie Ursillo's sister remarked, "He does, doesn't he?"

"Yes, he does. The eyes. It's eerie," the other girl agreed.

Abel didn't know what they were talking and didn't care. The Ursillo sister explained. "My sister said you had eyes like James Dean, that terrific actor who died a long time ago. He had the dreamiest eyes. I saw his picture. And you do too."

"Thanks, I guess," Abel replied. "Hey, would you girls do me a big favor? My little sister is in the dressing room trying on jeans. When she comes out, will you tell her she looks great in whatever she picks out?"

"Sure," the girls agreed, giggling again.

Penelope emerged in a few minutes. "This is an eight," she announced. "Does it look okay?"

"Oh, girl!" Cassie's sister responded. "You look hot!"

Penelope looked surprised. She smiled and said, "Really?"

"Girl, you buy those jeans!" the other girl commanded.

Penelope beamed. After the girls were gone, she asked Abel, "Who were those nice girls?"

"Who knows?" Abel said. "Buy the jeans, and let's get out of here."

As the sunny day was fading and turning to dusk, they headed home to Sparrow Street and the Ruiz house.

"Thanks for putting that twenty to my money, Abel," Penelope said. "I couldn't have gotten the jeans if you hadn't done that. Thanks a lot. Wow, I really love those jeans. Do you think I looked okay?"

"Super!" Abel told her. Actually, he thought, she didn't look bad at all in them.

As he turned on Sparrow Street, he spotted Tomás's Honda in the driveway. In the driveway themselves, Abel turned to his sister. "Now, lissen up, Penny," he ordered. "He's only gonna be here for a day and a half. It means a lot to Mom to have everything good. We can keep our cool for a day and a half. The big windbag'll blow out of here tomorrow night, okay? Let's not give Mom one of her headaches. We don't want to ruin her visit from Prince Charming."

Penelope giggled. "You're lots nicer than you usually are, Abel," she remarked.

"It's maturity, kid," Abel stated solemnly. "Old age is creeping up on me. I'm having my eighteenth birthday in a coupla months. From then on, it's downhill all the way."

"Hey, there they are!" Tomás shouted as the front door opened, admitting Abel and Penelope. "My beautiful little sister and my handsome kid brother!" He grabbed Penelope for a hug and a kiss. Abel hoped against hope for just a brotherly handshake, but Tomás hugged him too.

"Well, Tomás, everything wonderful with you as usual?" Abel asked, trying not to sound bitter.

"I got this award for being the most promising dude in the sophomore class," Tomás answered. Tomás picked up the parchment in the walnut frame and waved it, almost hitting Abel in the nose. "Hey, Abel," Tomás continued, "Mom was just telling me that the girl you were going with—that Claudia chick. She dumped you? Hey, man, that's too bad."

Abel glanced at his mother. He hoped she'd see the rage in his eyes, but she probably didn't. "Why does she humiliate me like this?" he thought.

"Well," Tomás rattled on, "don't sweat it, man. Chicks can be a pain. I've been going with this amazing girl, Zoe. Smart, gorgeous, on the honor roll like me. Just so fun to be with. I bought her a ruby pendant for her birthday. I spent a fortune on her, but I thought she was worth it."

"Ohhh!" Mom moaned in delight. "That's the girl whose pictures you put on your Facebook page, you and her at the county fair. What a lovely girl. You looked so good together. Tomás, you must bring her—"

Tomás plopped down in the big leather chair, crossed his legs, and held his hand up, palm facing Mom. "She tweeted me on my way down here. She found somebody else," he announced.

A deep, almost unbelievable silence fell over the living room. Mom's eyes seemed as large as dinner plates. Abel was sure he misunderstood what Tomás had said, but then he got it. It had to be a joke, he figured. Tomás was making fun of him for being dumped by Claudia. Tomás was pretending that he, too, had been dumped. It was a sadistic joke on Abel.

"What did you say, Tomás?" Penelope asked, breaking the silence. "Some girl dumped *you*?"

"Yeah," Tomás confirmed. "Zoe Fernandez. Dumped me like a hot potato."

"Oh, Tomás," Mom cried in a grief–stricken voice. "I am so sorry. Oh, my poor boy. How could she do such a thing!"

"It's okay, Mom," Tomás assured her. "It's not the end of the world. It hurts my pride, and, sure, I feel bad. But she wasn't for me, that's all. Better we found it out now. That Claudia wasn't for you either, Abel. We're both too young to settle on one chick anyway, bro. This is the time to enjoy life."

He turned then to Penelope and remarked, "When did you get to be so pretty, *hermana*? But, listen, you need to put on a little weight. You're too skinny. *Muchachos* like curves, right, Abel?"

Both Abel and Penelope were flooded with an emotion neither of them often felt for their brother—affection. Abel had not planned to cook a meal for Tomás while he was here. They planned to go out for dinner tomorrow. But now Abel announced, "Tomás, I'm cooking something special tomorrow, just for you. I want you to see what a fine chef I've become!"

That Sunday evening. Ernesto Sandoval and Naomi Martinez were driving past Cesar Chavez High School. They saw a small group of freshman standing around, and they looked as though they might be trouble.

"I don't see gang colors, Naomi. But I don't like how those dudes are just standing around staring at the school," Ernesto observed. "This might be the bunch who went in and spray painted the library.

They might be wannabe gangbangers trying to prove themselves. One of them looks familiar, but I don't know the dude's name."

Ernesto pulled to the curb and shouted out the window, "Hey, homies, what's goin' down?"

"Nothin', man," the tallest of the group shot back.

"Four dudes just standing around the school on a Sunday night," Ernesto commented. "Doesn't look good to me. If a police cruiser came around the corner just about now, you guys might have some explaining to do."

"Oh, the tall one is Rocky Salcedo," Naomi told Ernesto. "That's the guy who looked familiar. He's been in trouble."

"Hey, Rocky!" Ernesto called out. "You better be getting on home."

The boy looked startled that the senior guy knew his name. He muttered something to his friends, and they all ambled on down the street.

"Know what?" Ernesto remarked. "I got a bad feeling that those dudes were up to something. My Uncle Arturo knows a really good cop who's savvy about the *barrio*, Jerry Davis. I think I'll text Uncle Arturo to tip off his friend. Maybe they could send a cruiser around to the school. The punks might be coming back. If they see police action, it could discourage them from whatever they have in mind."

Within fifteen minutes of Ernesto's text to his uncle, a police cruiser appeared on Washington Street in front of the high school. *Tío* Arturo must have called his friend at home. The four boys were now standing across the street. The cruiser stopped there, and two officers got out to talk to them. Within minutes, the boys were sitting on the curb talking to the officers.

Naomi looked worried. "I hope those guys don't connect you talking to them and the police coming around," she said.

"Yeah, well, I'd kick myself if Chavez was vandalized tonight," Ernesto responded. "If I'd seen suspicious-looking dudes and done nothing, I'd be laying awake at night. Getting a visit from the police might discourage them."

"I've heard that Rocky Salcedo is a tough kid and a poor student," Naomi remarked. "But what good would spray painting the library do for him?"

"Who knows?" Ernesto replied. "Rocky's a freshman, but he looks at least fifteen. I think he's been held back one grade at least. He's probably really frustrated. Mad at the world. Sometimes people just lash out."

The police got back into the cruiser, and Ernesto and Naomi went home.

When Ernesto got home, he finished his AP project from Mr. Bustos, and that was a great relief. Ernesto was leaning back in his chair and taking a deep breath when his cell rang.

"Ernie," Naomi cried, "check out your Facebook page. Somebody's posting awful pictures of Mr. Davila! I don't know if they got to your page, but the pictures've gone viral. Everybody's getting them!"

"What?" Ernesto gasped. He checked his Facebook page on his iPad and found pictures taken of Jesse Davila at embarrassing moments. Somebody from his classes must have had an iPhone and had taken pictures when Mr. Davila was misspeaking or just looking silly. They caught him during a sneezing spell that was hilarious but humiliating. One day last week, Mr. Davila's briefcase popped open, and his papers flew all over. The page showed pictures of him scrambling around the floor retrieving his stuff. All together, the pictures made Jesse Davila look like a laughable fool, not a teacher to be respected.

"Oh man! Who did this?" Ernesto groaned.

"It's awful, Ernie," Naomi responded. "I'm sure these horrible pictures have been sent to the other teachers, the administration. It's like character assassination. Maybe some creep just put the pictures on their own Facebook page and sent them to friends. And they sent it on to somebody else and . . . it just went viral."

"How do you stop something like this?" Ernesto exclaimed. He didn't expect an answer. There was no answer. It could happen to anybody.

"It's like that lady sportswriter," Naomi responded. "Some freak snapped pictures of her through a hole in her hotel room and put it out there. She was just devastated."

"Yeah," Ernesto added, "every iPhone's a camera now. It's not only that Big Brother's watching you. It's worse. Somebody can destroy you with a click on an iPhone. It's worse than like getting mugged or beat up. Or even having your house robbed. Man, it's like somebody takes your . . . dignity."

Naomi nodded in agreement.

"I'm thinking Rod Garcia," Naomi guessed. "He's been so down on Mr. Davila. But how can you prove it?"

"Yeah," Ernesto agreed. "Remember the other day when Mrs. Sanchez came in to observe, and we all made Mr. Davila look good? Rod stopped me and told me he wasn't done yet. He planned to get rid of Mr. Davila."

"It's enough to make you want to smash all the iPhones," Naomi fumed, "and go back to the old-fashioned phones. Imagine how hard this is going to be on Angel Roma. She's under enough stress already. Some mean kids've been making fun of her taking care of her sick grandmother. Now her grandfather is made to look like a fool. It's like terrorism, Ernie."

"I know," Ernesto agreed. "What can we do, though? Do you think we should call Mr. Davila and . . . " Ernesto's voice trailed off. What could they possibly say that would make any difference? "We're sorry about those horrible pictures of you,

Mr. Davila. We want to express out outrage that such an evil thing was done." Lame. But both Ernesto and Naomi knew saying something like that would only make matters worse.

"Poor Mr. Davila," Ernesto groaned. "Taking care of a sick wife and having a daughter and granddaughter living with him. How much piling on can the poor guy take? And he's a Vietnam veteran too. He served his country, and he's a good teacher. It's so not right, and yet there's nothing we can do."

When Ernesto saw Rod Garcia on Monday morning, he walked over to him and spoke coldly. "You must have gotten a big laugh over those stupid pictures of Mr. Davila. You wouldn't have had anything to do with that happening, would you?"

"I've seen them, sure, but I didn't take the pictures and put them out there," Rod insisted. "Somebody in class did it, but not me. But the pictures tell the story, don't they? The guy is clearly an idiot who doesn't belong in the classroom. Like that old saying, 'A picture is worth a thousand words.'" Garcia's face wore a pleased smirk.

"Whoever did this is one evil dude," Ernesto said.

"I don't see it that way, man," Garcia objected. "Wake up, Sandoval. The time is past when we have to put up with old, incompetent teachers. Times are changing. The old fogies and their outdated methods are done. Tenure for lousy teachers! Ha! That's going out like the dinosaurs, man. Get with it."

"Mr. Davila is an excellent teacher," Ernesto asserted. "On the teacher evaluation form the students fill out, he's one of the best here at Chavez."

"Yeah?" Rod sneered. "Maybe that says a lot about how crummy the whole faculty is, dude. Maybe your father isn't such a hot teacher either. Jelly brains like you might put up with bad teachers out of some lamebrained idea of compassion. But you're screwing the rest of us, dude. Compassion don't cut it anymore. We gotta go out in the world and be well educated to get a good job. We count. The students count. When a car gets old, we junk it and send it to the crusher, Sandoval. You don't keep on trying to drive a busted car. That old dude won't get out of the way on his own. So maybe somebody needs to spread the word any way they can that he has to go."

As Rod Garcia walked away, he fired a parting shot. "You're going outta style with your sappy attitude, Sandoval. We're the future."

Ernesto stared at the other boy and shouted at Rod's back. "If you're the future, dude, we're all in trouble."

CHAPTER FIVE

Ernesto had signed up for the ninth-grade big brother, big sister program and got a boy named Richie Loranzo. The boy's story was shocking. He was living in a foster home in the *barrio* since last year. That was when, in a horrific case of domestic violence, his father fatally shot his mother. The father was now in prison. The boy had no extended family, so he was placed in a foster home. Ernesto learned that the boy was painfully shy and did not relate well to anybody. Ernesto could only imagine what life had been like in the Loranzo home even before the tragic death of Richie's mother. Deadly domestic violence usually occurred after months or years of brutality. Richie may have witnessed terrible events.

Ernesto, Abel, and Naomi had planned a trip for their three freshmen on the next Saturday. They were going into the mountains for an all-day adventure, with Abel packing the lunches. Ernesto and Naomi kicked in to buy the food that Abel needed. With Abel making the food, Ernesto knew that at least that part of the day—lunch— would be a big success.

Ernesto borrowed his friend's van, which comfortably fit all six students. Cruz Lopez was happy to lend his gaudily decorated van, and the sight of it was a big hit with the freshmen.

Ernesto drove with Richie beside him. Abel, Bobby Padilla, Naomi, and Angel Roma sat in the backseats.

"So, Richie," Ernesto asked as they started out, "how's ninth grade going so far?"

Richie stared straight ahead. "Okay," he replied. He looked like someone who had seen a ghost. He had looked that way ever since his terrible experience. He was still stunned.

"I didn't like ninth grade," Ernesto remarked. "I hated to leave middle school. Lotsa creepy kids in ninth grade. They think they're big shots or something."

"Yeah," Angel Roma agreed. "I hate most of the kids in my classes."

"I got a coupla friends," Bobby Padilla chimed in. "One guy's got a real cool iPhone, and he lets me play with it."

"You ever been up in the mountains before, you guys?" Abel asked the three ninth-graders.

"I never was," Bobby answered. "Mom drives, but she's scared of driving in the mountains."

"Me neither," Richie said. "Are there wild animals in the mountains?"

"Maybe some mule deer, rabbits," Ernesto responded. "We gotta watch out for rattlesnakes. Don't step anywhere where you can't see. Rattlers don't bother you if you don't bother them, but it's easy to step on one by mistake."

"Snakes are cool," Bobby Padilla commented.

"I hate them," Angel Roma said.

The road became more twisted as they went higher in the mountains. "Notice how green it gets up here," Naomi pointed. "In the foothills, it's kinda yellow, but now it's lush green. That's because we get more rain in the mountains."

"Here's a good place to have lunch," Ernesto suggested. Ernesto parked, and they all got out.

Bobby Padilla looked around, brightening when he saw the white flash of a cottontail rabbit. "Did you guys see that?" he asked.

"I love rabbits," Angel remarked. "Sometimes they come in our yard. They eat the vegetables Grandpa plants, but he doesn't mind. Grandma used to plant tomatoes before she got really sick. They tasted lots better than the ones you buy in the store."

"What's your grandma sick with?" Richie asked, showing his first real sign of interest since the trip began.

"She's got Parkinson's disease," Angela answered. "She walks kinda funny, and she can't talk good anymore. Sometimes mean kids laugh at her."

"I wouldn't laugh at her," Richie said. He had a serious, almost grim look on his face. "I never would."

Angel Roma had seen Richie in her classes at Chavez. He always hung his head and didn't look at anybody. She thought something was wrong with him. But now she thought he was a nice-looking boy with his curly black hair and chin dimple. She thought he would be a lot cuter if he smiled more, which he usually didn't.

"I have to help my Grandma and take her for walks 'cause the doctor said she'd get even worse if she didn't exercise," Angel explained. "Sometimes these girls walk behind us and imitate Grandma, and I feel awful. I'm so embarrassed."

84

"I bet that makes Grandma feel bad too," Bobby remarked.

"I guess," Angel replied, "but she doesn't say much. But I get red in the face, and I want to cry. The girls who mock us—me and Gram—they're in my class at school. That's why I hate school so much."

"Who are the girls who make fun of you and your grandma, Angel?" Naomi was asking gently, as she carried one of the picnic baskets toward the little stream.

"Lacey Serrano is the worst," Angel answered. "Coupla days ago, she was telling everybody that both my grandparents are weird. She said there were terrible pictures of my grandpa online, and she laughed and laughed. I wish I could hit her so hard that she'd never wake up."

Naomi exchanged looks with Ernesto.

"You know what?" Richie declared suddenly, startling everybody by jumping into the conversation. "When they laugh at your grandma, you should laugh too. And your grandma should laugh too. Then it won't be fun for them to laugh at you 'cause everybody'll be laughing."

"I don't know," Angel responded. "I don't think I could do that." But Angel smiled at Richie. She knew he was really trying to help, and she appreciated that.

Abel had a large, puffy chef's hat with him. When he put it on, Angel and Bobby laughed, and even Richie managed to smile. Abel had brought an ice chest with cold drinks and the fillings for the sandwiches. He was making the sandwiches fresh, on the spot.

"Who wants sliced turkey and who wants ham?" Abel asked, taking everybody's order. Then he started assembling the sandwiches, cheese, pickles, olive slices, and slivers of avocado and pepper. He topped them all of with a special kind of mayo that he mixed himself.

"These are sooo good," Ernesto commented as he tasted his turkey sandwich.

"Of course," Abel agreed. "I'm a chef."

CHAPTER FIVE

Bobbie and Angel raved about the sandwiches, and so did Naomi. Richie showed how much he liked his ham sandwich by wolfing it down. Then they all had slices of homemade apple pie and cold drinks.

Bobbie stopped munching on his sandwich long enough to ask Abel how he got so good at making sandwiches.

"Ernesto got me goin'," Abel replied. "He got me to get after my dream of cooking. I work at the Sting Ray, and my boss says I'm good. I think I am too. . . . And I made this dinner for my brother. He loved it. That doesn't sound like much, maybe. But my mom, she's nuts about my older brother. He's a god to her. I'm the goof-off to her. Anyway, he couldn't get over how good the meal was. And he told me that. That meant a lot to me."

Abel looked off into the distance. "Yeah," he added, "a lot."

"Well," Bobbie responded, gulping down a bite of his lunch, "whatever you put on this sandwich is super!"

A little after lunch, the three seniors went off with their freshman buddies in different directions.

Ernesto walked along the stream with Richie. "Want to take off your shoes and socks and wade in the water?" Ernesto asked.

"You gonna?" Richie asked.

"Yeah," Ernesto said. "It's kinda warm now, and the cold water'll feel good."

They sat down on rocks and pulled off their shoes and socks, stacking them carefully against a tree trunk.

They stepped into the little stream, walking carefully on the smooth stones in the stream bed. After a while, they sat in the grass, their feet still in the water.

"Richie," Ernesto asked, "are your foster parents nice?" He was thinking about his friends, Paul and David Morales. They'd grown up in foster homes and had a lot of bad times. Most of the people who took in foster children did their best. But it was hard to form a real attachment to kids who kept coming and going.

"Yeah," Richie replied.

"Do they have kids of their own?" Ernesto asked.

"They're kinda old. Their kids are gone," Richie answered.

"Do you like them, Richie?" Ernesto asked.

Richie shrugged. "They're okay," he said. Richie swished his bare feet in the water and watched the ripples form. For a few seconds, the boy said nothing. Then he set his jaw, and his eyes narrowed. "They said on TV that Daddy was a monster. He wasn't, though. He took me fishing on the bay. Once I caught a big fish. It was fun on the boat," Richie recalled.

Ernesto felt his heart racing. He wasn't sure how to deal with a tragedy as profound as this kid was dealing with. Ernesto had no idea what had happened to bring about such an awful event. Nothing could justify what the father did. But still that kind of thing happened all too frequently. Married people fought violently, and then—

suddenly—things escalated in a terrible way. Ernesto's mouth was dry. He didn't know what he could say to the sad-eyed boy that would make things any better.

"She's nice," Richie declared suddenly. He glanced over to where Naomi and Angel were looking through the binoculars that Naomi had brought. They were focusing on a distant tree.

"Who's nice, Richie?" Ernesto asked softly. He was relieved that the subject changed.

"Angel Roma," the boy answered. "She's in my history class. One time I forgot my lunch, and she cut her sandwich in half. She cut her peach in half too and shared it with me. I hate it when kids are mean to her 'cause her grandma walks funny."

"Yeah," Ernesto agreed. Then he had an idea. "I wonder what Naomi and Angel see up in the tree."

Ernesto and Richie went back to where their socks and shoes were stacked. They put them back on and joined the two girls. By now, Abel and Bobby were there too. Naomi turned to Ernesto and said, "It's an eagle—"

"Two of them!" Angel added excitedly.

Naomi gave everybody a turn on the binoculars until they all saw the eagles. "They're bald eagles. They were endangered for a long time," Naomi explained. "But now they're thriving. That's so exciting that we saw them. You guys can tell your friends at school on Monday that you saw two bald eagles. I got some cool pictures for you on my iPhone. I think I can blow them up and sharpen them on my computer."

Before they headed home in the late afternoon, they took one more walk. The seniors and their ninth-graders switched places with one other. Ernesto took Angel, and Abel took Richie. Naomi walked with Bobby Padilla.

"Richie said you were nice, Angel," Ernesto remarked.

Angel turned and stared at Ernesto. "No!" she insisted. "Nobody likes me 'cept for Penny Ruiz. I think he just feels sorry for me. Nobody wants to be with me. That's 'cause Lacey's telling everybody I'm gonna start walking funny and talking weird like my grandma pretty soon."

"Hey, all I know is Richie said you're nice," Ernesto repeated. "He said you shared your lunch with him."

"Yeah," Angel admitted. She looked intently at Ernesto, "Did he *really* say I was nice?"

"Yeah, he did, Angel," Ernesto replied. "And you *are* nice."

Angel looked pensive. "None of us got dads," she commented. "My dad ran away, and so did Bobby's. Richie's dad is in jail. I asked Richie once if he hated his dad, and he said he didn't. I would hate somebody who hurt my mom. I would hate them so much. I'd sneak up behind them one day and hit them hard on the head until they were dead."

"*Ay, muchacha!*" Ernesto responded softly. "You have a lot of anger in you. You

92

need to let it go. It makes you sick when you hate people. I know you have the right to be really mad at those mean girls who make fun of you and your grandma. But don't let them fill your heart with hatred. Hate always makes you sick, and it doesn't bother the one you hate."

Angel looked right at Ernesto. "I want to make Lacey Serrano hurt. I get so mad when she mocks me and Grandma that I feel like exploding in a million pieces. Didn't you ever hate somebody so much that you wanted to hurt them?"

"Yes, Angel, I know what you're talking about," Ernesto responded. "But I tried to fight off the hatred. You're doing a very kind and brave thing to take your grandmother for walks. You're a hero for doing that. A lotta kids just wouldn't do it. They'd be too selfish. So you're a special girl, Angel."

Ernesto wasn't sure he was getting through to the girl. "Someday," he went on, "you'll look back on how you helped your grandmother, and you'll be proud of what you did. You'll feel good. When you do a kind and brave thing, it's hard at the time. But for all your life, it will comfort you that you did it."

Tears filled Angel's eyes. "Why do they make fun of Grandma and Grandpa? Grandma doesn't want to be sick, and Grandpa is trying to be a good teacher."

"Angel, your grandfather is my history teacher, and he's a fine teacher," Ernesto assured the girl. "Most of his students like him a lot. I'm learning so much in that class. Your grandfather is smart and interesting. You know my dad teaches history at Chavez, right? Well, he says the same things about your grandfather. Dad admires him,"

"When the bad pictures came online, Grandpa cried," Angel confided. "He told me he wasn't crying. He said he got dust in his eye. But I *knew* he was crying. He didn't want us to see the pictures, but Mom and I saw them. It was so awful. Mom doesn't make much money on her job. If they fire Grandpa, our family's gonna be in trouble. Maybe we couldn't even stay in our house. Grandpa was gonna retire. But then when Mom and me came to live with him, he said he'd keep on teaching to take care of us. Grandpa took us in."

"Well, Angel, pretty soon everybody is going to forget the bad pictures," Ernesto said, consoling her. "They'll only remember what a good teacher your grandfather is. Know what, Angel? On the way home, we're gonna stop for ice cream sundaes. Does that sound good?"

"Yeah!" Angel responded. "I want lotsa nuts and syrup on mine."

"And gobs of whipped cream," Ernesto added, smiling.

Much later, Ernesto dropped the ninth-graders off at their homes, filled with butterscotch and chocolate ice cream sundaes. When it was just the three seniors in the van, Ernesto reflected on the day. He said to Abel and Naomi, "I feel good about today.

95

I think the kids really had fun, and it kinda gave us all a chance to know each other better. The kids could push their problems out of the way for a little while and just have fun. And it gave them the chance to talk too."

"I talked to Richie's foster mother when she signed him up for this program, Ernie," Naomi responded. "She told me he never said a word about what happened to his parents. She said he's like locked up in a painful little bubble, and he won't open up at all. But today when you guys were wading in the stream, I saw you talking quite a bit, and that made me happy. I think you have a buddy there."

"Yeah, I think we made some progress," Ernesto agreed. "It's so hard for a kid like that to get past what happened. I just can't imagine what he's going through."

"Bobby had a lot of fun," Abel piped up. "I told him I'd come over to his house sometime and show his mother how to make cream puffs. Bobby loves cream puffs. His Mom tried to make 'em a coupla times, but they didn't get puffy. They went flat like pancakes. He was really excited that I'd come over and show her how to do it. I like the kid. I mean, I'm gettin' as much from him as he's gettin' from me, maybe more."

Naomi looked thoughtful. She looked at Ernesto and said, "I'm worried about Angel. Did you catch how angry she is? I mean, I understand it, but . . ."

"Yeah, I hear you," Ernesto agreed. "I tried to tell her that hating just ends up hurting you more than whoever you hate. But I don't think I got through to her. We've got to find a way to stop those kids who're hassling her. I'm not sure how, but bullying like that can't just go on."

That evening, when Ernesto got home, his father had news. "They may have found out who vandalized the school," Dad reported. "Mrs. Sanchez called me and said there was solid evidence against a student."

CHAPTER SIX

As Ernesto Sandoval came on campus Monday morning, he noticed a group of girls. They were gathered around one freshman girl in particular. A couple of them were crying, and the one who seemed to be the center of attention was hysterical. Ernesto didn't know the girl who was freaking out. Then Penelope Ruiz came walking over. Her brother Abel had just dropped her off.

"Hey, Penelope," Ernesto called, "what's going on over there?"

Penelope laughed harshly. "That's Lacey Serrano having the crying jag," she answered. "She tweeted everybody that she's getting blamed for spray painting the library. She says she didn't do it, of course. She's going ballistic, huh? It couldn't happen to a bigger creep. She hangs with that gross Rocky Salcedo, who's always calling me fat. I bet he was in on it too."

Ernesto and Penelope stared at Lacey for a few seconds. Then Penelope shook her head and spoke. "Oh, I hope they get so busted! I hope Lacey and Rocky get grounded for the rest of their lives. I hope their stupid parents take away their iPhones and their laptops and their mattresses too. I hope they make them sleep on the floor."

"Penny, calm down," Ernesto advised, trying not to grin. "Why would Lacey Serrano do such a thing? Spray painting dirty words on the library wall? I mean, she's a good student, isn't she?"

"Oh, she cheats like crazy, but Mr. Lucas is so clueless," Penelope explained. "She turned in a paper the other day about the crisis in Africa. Even *I* knew she copied it online. Lucas gave her an A. Can you believe it? Lacey's so mean to poor Angel and her sick grandmother. What kinda creep would make fun of a sick old lady and the kid who's helping her walk? I mean, is that the lowest thing you ever heard of, Ernie?"

Penelope finally stopped to take a breath, but she soon continued her rant. "I read a fairy tale once about a mean girl who plucked the wings off of insects. Then one day she fell into a pit, and she was buried to her neck. All the bugs came and tormented her. The spiders and wasps, all came and feasted on her head. That's what should happen to Lacey."

"Wow!" Ernesto exclaimed. "Remind me to never get on your bad side, Penny."

"Oh, Ernie," Penelope responded, "you're the best. You could never get on my bad side. Abel just loves you. He said you're the best friend a guy ever had."

Even while she was talking to Ernesto, Penelope's eyes were locked on Lacey Serrano. Penelope started laughing. "Look at her bawling like a baby! She runs after Angel and taunts her. Now that something bad happens to her, she acts like a two-year-old!"

Finally, Lacey Serrano began walking to her class, still sobbing. Her best friend, Candy Tellez, walked beside her, comforting her, her arm around Lacey's shoulders.

By lunchtime, the story was all around the school. Bits and pieces were texted and tweeted. Somehow the school administration had been tipped off to check Lacey Serrano's locker. There, tucked in the back, was a can of spray paint of the exact shade as that used in the vandalism. Lacey Serrano was now a person of interest in the crime.

Lacey and her mother had been asked to meet with the principal Monday morning to explain the can of paint in her locker. That paint was the only evidence against Lacey. It was of the same rare purple color that had been used to spray paint the library wall.

At that meeting, Lacey could not say what the paint was doing in her locker. And she vehemently denied vandalizing the library. Her mother came with her to the interview. Mrs. Serrano threatened legal action against the school if her innocent daughter's reputation was damaged.

During the interview, Mrs. Serrano had become very emotional. "Some vile child planted the spray can in my daughter's locker," she screamed. "Then told you it was there. My poor little girl is the victim of a frame-up."

Mrs. Sanchez kept her cool despite all the emotion.

And after the meeting, Lacey Serrano texted all her friends with details of her "ordeal."

"I wonder who tipped the school to check Lacey's locker?" Naomi remarked to the other kids at lunch.

"I heard it was an anonymous tip," Julio Avila replied. Julio was on the track team with Ernesto.

"I'm just wondering how she was stupid enough to keep the spray paint right in her locker," Ernesto commented. "You'd think she woulda dumped the can somewhere far from here."

"It sounds weird," Abel agreed. "Lacey's got a lot of enemies 'cause she's so mean, but, still, something doesn't add up here."

Julio Avila laughed. "From what I hear, this kid is bad to the bone. Seems like, whatever happened, she's got it comin'." Julio leaned back on the grass and chomped on his apple. "I hope she gets keelhauled good."

"What's 'keelhauled'?" Abel asked.

"My old man was a sailor," Julio explained. His father was an alcoholic and a loser too. But he was the only family Julio had, and Julio loved him. Julio knew what it was like to be mocked by cruel classmates. When his disheveled father would show up at school, Julio was ribbed without mercy. He knew what Angel Roma was going through. "Keelhauling is punishin' somebody by dragging them under a ship. They'd get all scraped up by the barnacles stickin' to the hull. Sounds good to me."

When Ernesto Sandoval came onto the field for track practice, Rod Garcia hadn't arrived yet. The ill will between the boys was no secret. Coach Muñoz liked his track team members to be buddies or at least to respect one another, especially in the relay races. Guys who hate each other can't be handing off the baton to one another. Making the other guy look bad could become more important than helping the team win.

Coach Muñoz approached Ernesto with a serious look on his face. "Sandoval, you and Garcia have a problem that worries me for the sake of the team."

"Don't worry, Coach," Ernesto assured him. "Whatever problems we have, I won't bring them on the track."

"I don't know what beef you guys have, and I don't want to know," Coach Muñoz said. "All I care about is the team."

Coach Muñoz was single-minded. All he cared about was winning the championship this year. He hadn't paid any attention to the senior class president election. He

104

had no idea that Ernesto had beaten Garcia out of the job he wanted so badly. Coach Muñoz didn't know that Rod was leading the charge to destroy poor Mr. Davila, the beleaguered history teacher. Ernesto saw nothing to be gained by exposing all that. Ernesto was happy just to follow the Coach's wishes. Coach didn't want to know what was going on between Ernesto and Rod.

"Nothing's going to interfere with taking the Cougars to another championship, Coach," Ernesto vowed. Last year, the Cesar Chavez Cougars track team won the regional championships. A lot of the credit went to Julio Avila, who had developed amazing speed in the last year and a half.

Julio was not running for just the glory of the team. He wasn't running just for his own pride. His father never failed to watch the races, and the only bright spot in the man's life was his son's triumphs. Julio hoped to do well enough this year to win an athletic scholarship to college and go on to compete in the Olympic trials. Julio had an ultimate fantasy. He'd be standing on that Olympic stage as they played the national anthem, the gold medal around his neck. He'd look out at the crowd and see his father standing there proudly. Julio knew that, if that ever happened, he wouldn't see anybody else in the crowd. All he'd see is one decrepit old man who would be crying tears of joy.

The rest of the team arrived and went through their warm-ups, including Rod Garcia. Garcia knew better than to start anything in front of Coach Muñoz, but he cast a dirty look at Ernesto.

Ernesto liked all the other guys on the team, especially Jorge Aguilar and Eddie Gonzales. A few weeks ago, Jorge had started hanging with gangbangers. Ernesto risked his life to rescue him. Now Jorge was back on the team and in classes.

"Okay," Coach Muñoz announced, toying a little nervously his timer. "Let's see what you boys got."

The whole team started from the blocks. Rod Garcia took the lead. Ernesto was just behind him, and Julio was in third place. Jorge and Eddie were taking the fourth and fifth spots.

Ernesto had been spending a lot of time running and doing stretching exercises. He was disappointed that he wasn't faster. He wanted to catch and pass Garcia. But from the corner of his eye, Ernesto saw Julio coming on like never before. Julio had always been fast, but today he was amazing. He flew past Ernesto and then Garcia. He put so much distance between himself and Garcia, who remained second, that it was no contest.

"Avila," Coach Muñoz exclaimed, "you are incredible!"

Julio Avila grinned. "Coach, I been running twenty miles every day and running sprints up and down my street," he explained. "I get up at four in the morning to run and do six miles. Then, before school, I do another six. I get in the other eight miles and sprints at night."

"You guys," Coach Muñoz declared in a nearly worshipful voice, "you see what dedication can do?"

At the end of practice, the boys were walking from the practice field. Rod Garcia caught up to Ernesto. "I put you in the shade, man," he boasted.

Ernesto decided to ignore Garcia. He kept walking.

"I'll beat Avila next time too," Garcia swore. "I plan to break a world record on this team and qualify for the Olympic trials."

"Dream on, man," Ernesto finally remarked. "Julio's the best I've ever seen. If anybody from Cesar Chavez High gets to the Olympics, it's gonna be Julio."

"That little punk?" Garcia sneered. "My father was a track star in college. It's in my genes. You ever see Avila's father? He's a drunken bum. No way he passed decent genes down to that little punk son of his."

Ernesto laughed and stopped walking. He just couldn't let such a stupid comment go unanswered. "I never heard of championship genes, dude. Look at the great runners in sports history. Never heard that Usain Bolt's dad was a champion. Never heard of Michael Johnson or Wilson Kipketer having a dad who excelled in running. That's all nonsense. Julio's got a real shot at the Olympics, and I'm rooting for him."

Before Rod Garcia could respond, Ernesto wheeled and jogged toward the locker room.

The next morning, Ernesto met Naomi and Carmen on the way to classes.

"Ernie," Naomi said excitedly. "Something so cool has happened! You know, since we took Bobby and Richie and Angel on that trip into the mountains, they've become friends! They hang out together at lunch now, and they never did that before. They got a little lunch gang now, like we do, Ernie. At lunchtime they'd mostly eat alone, and now they're buddies!"

"That's super," Ernesto responded.

"Penelope's part of the group too," Naomi continued. "She's such a sweetheart. She gets Abel to make stuff, and she treats everybody sometimes. Penelope is sorta the leader. Oh, Ernie, it's so important for kids like that to have a support system!"

"Isn't that so great, Ernie?" Carmen asked. "You know, kids are sorta like wild animals. I saw a TV show about the elephants and the wildebeest in Africa. If they all stick together, then they're safe from their enemies. On this show, the elephants and the wildebeest formed a circle. They stood there in a big group against the lions who were coming to attack them. That's just like those mean kids. They can't pick on you if you've got friends. By themselves, those four kids are like natural outsiders, easy prey for the bullies. But together, they can't be beat!"

Ernesto laughed. "You're right, Carmen," he agreed. "I always thought school was sorta like living in the wild. The big mean students prey on the weaker ones. Guys like Clay and Rod, girls like Lacey and Candy. The good kids gotta band together against them, like those elephants and the wildebeest."

Naomi changed the subject. "I wonder if Lacey *is* the one who spray painted the library," she asked. "It seems strange, but . . ."

"She's mean, but she's sly too," Carmen noted. "I don't buy it. She woulda lost the spray can."

"You think she's been set up?" Ernesto asked.

Naomi shrugged. "My mom sorta knows her mother. Mrs. Serrano and Mom work on the PTA together sometimes. Mrs. Serrano is really freaking out over this. She swore up and down that Lacey would never do such a thing. She thinks it's some evil plot against her poor little innocent angel of a daughter."

"Naomi, does Mrs. Serrano have *any* idea of the kind of stuff her kid does around school or on the street?" Ernesto asked. "Does this lady know what Lacey does to Angel Roma and her grandmother? Do you think she knows Lacey and her friend walk behind them making fun of the old lady's disability?"

A sad look came to Naomi's face, but Carmen looked furious. "Ernie, do they really do that?' Carmen demanded.

"Angel said they do, and I believe her," Ernesto answered.

"I'm going over to the Serrano house after school today and tell her parents," Carmen declared in a shrill voice. "Do you guys know where they live?"

Ernesto grabbed his cell phone. "I'm calling your mom, Naomi. She'd know," he said. He got the address quickly from Linda Martinez.

"They live on Cardinal Street," Ernesto reported. "Those nice new condos."

Carmen had a determined look on her face. "Well, Mrs. Serrano is in for a rude awakening!" Carmen glanced at her friends. "Anybody brave enough to come with me? If not, I'll go alone."

CHAPTER SIX

"I would," Naomi replied. "But I gotta get home right after school. Mom 'has a doctor's appointment, and I'm going to drive her. She usually drives. But she's so nervous about this appointment that she'd feel better if I drove. It's a mammogram, and she freaks out whenever she has one of those."

"I'll go," Ernesto responded. He wasn't looking forward to it, but he admired Carmen's determination to do the right thing. He wasn't about to let her go alone. Carmen was her father's daughter all right. Emilio Zapata Ibarra had run for the city council and won so that he could help the people of the *barrio*. He wanted to erase corruption and bring justice. So far, he had made great strides.

At the end of the school day, Ernesto drove Carmen in his Volvo.

Cardinal Street had nice houses, some of the nicest in the *barrio* and some of them built thirty or forty years ago. Many were stucco with Spanish tile roofs. It also had middle-class apartments, like the one Paul and David Morales lived in, and sparkling new condos. The Serranos lived in one of the condos. Developers were slowly tearing down the single-family homes, as the owners grew too old to keep them up, and building fine condos in their place.

"There's the address Naomi's mom gave me," Ernesto pointed. "This must be it." He pulled into the parking area and stopped where a sign said "Visitors."

Ernesto and Carmen walked to the door of the unit. A few seconds after they rang the bell, an attractive woman came to the door. "Yes?" she asked in an annoyed voice. "If you're selling something, I don't want—"

"No, Mrs. Serrano," Carmen interrupted. Carmen had seen the woman bringing Lacey to school and knew what she looked like. "We have something very important to talk to you about. We're students at Cesar Chavez High School, and we really need to talk to you."

"Well, I'm very busy," Mrs. Serrano replied. "What is this about?"

Ernesto was starting to feel uneasy. The woman had a mean look on her face. In just a few seconds, Ernesto took an instant dislike to her. But he knew he had a duty to speak up and help Carmen with this. "Mrs. Serrano, it's about your daughter, Lacey. There have been things going on that you need to know about. May we come in for just a few minutes?"

Reluctantly, Mrs. Serrano stepped back and allowed them in. She looked at Ernesto and noted, "You're the senior class president at Chavez, aren't you?"

"Yes, ma'am, but this is about something else," Ernesto replied.

The woman ushered them into the living room. Both Carmen and Ernesto sat down in stiff, uncomfortable chairs. Mrs. Serrano sat across from them. She offered no refreshments, for which Ernesto was grateful. He couldn't have gotten anything down his throat.

"This is about your daughter, Lacey," Carmen began.

Rage filled the woman's eyes. "Have you come to apologize for the terrible way my child has been persecuted at the school?" she demanded. "Lacey is a wonderful girl, an excellent student. Now she's being falsely accused of that spray painting vandalism in the library. I have already talked to my lawyer. If the school continues to imply that my innocent child did this, they will be facing us in court."

"Mrs. Serrano," Carmen said in a strong voice, undaunted by the woman's wrath. "There is a girl in the freshman class who lives with a disabled grandmother. The woman has Parkinson's disease, and she staggers when she walks. The child lets her grandmother lean on her while they walk. Two freshmen girls from Chavez have been tormenting the girl and her grandmother by mockingly walking behind them and calling them names. Your daughter is one of those girls."

116

Mrs. Serrano rose up wrathfully in her chair, reminding Ernesto of a snake getting ready to strike. "How dare you come into my home and tell such contemptible lies about my daughter?" the woman demanded. "Lacey is a lovely, compassionate girl. She would never do such a terrible thing. I am outraged. Lacey is the kindest, sweetest child in the world. To suggest she would do something so loathsome is beyond contempt!"

"Mrs. Serrano, it's happening," Ernesto affirmed. "Your daughter is a bully, one of the mean girls at school. I'm not surprised that you know nothing about it or that Lacey has managed to fool you. I don't know anything about the spray painting incident, and maybe your daughter is innocent of that. But I do know that a little fourteen-year-old girl is being harassed every day by Lacey and her friend. We both think you need to talk to your daughter and convince her to stop."

"Get out of my home!" Mrs. Serrano screamed. "Or I will call the police! I am giving you two minutes to get out of my home, or you will be dealing with the police. Don't you dare *ever* come back here. And if you continue to spread lies about my child, my husband and I will sue you! And don't think we won't."

Carmen and Ernesto left the home immediately. As they went down the walk, Ernesto commented, "Whoa! The Wicked Witch of the West is alive and well."

"Like mother, like daughter," Carmen agreed bitterly.

CHAPTER SEVEN

L et's go over to Finch Street," Carmen suggested. "Angel Roma lives just a few doors from Jorge Aguilar. I bet the Aguilars have seen Angel walking with her grandmother. I know Jorge's sister, Elly. She's still in middle school, but she doesn't miss anything. I used to baby-sit her when she was younger."

Ernesto and Carmen stopped at the Aguilar house. Jorge came to the door. "Hey, Ernie, Carmen. Wassup?" he greeted. He seemed in a good mood.

"We're trying to find out about a family down a few doors," Ernesto replied. "A freshman from Chavez walks with her disabled grandmother and—"

"Oh yeah," Jorge interrupted. "Mr. Davila's wife. That old lady's in a bad way, man. The kid tries to lead her down the sidewalk, but sometimes it looks like the old lady is gonna take a header."

"Jorge, the girl who leads her grandmother," Carmen said, "she told us something. She said mean girls walk behind them and mock them and call them zombies. Do you know anything about that?"

"Oh yeah," Jorge responded. "It's pretty awful. The girls taunt Mrs. Davila and her granddaughter all the time. My sister Elly yells at them, but they just laugh. One time my mom yelled at them to stop. But then they called my mom names, you know, saying she's fat and stuff. Mom's a little overweight."

"Jorge, do you know who these girls are?" Ernesto asked.

Jorge turned and yelled inside the house, "Elly!" When the middle schooler came, Jorge said, "Sis, Ernie and Carmen want to know who those girls are who make fun of Mrs. Davila?"

"I'm gonna go to Chavez next year," Elly answered. "I'm gonna be a freshman. I know some of the kids already. There's this sorta pretty girl—she doesn't live around here, but she comes over sometimes. She's the one who makes fun of Mrs. Davila. She called my mom a dirty name too. She's gross. I don't know her last name, but her first name is Lacey. The girl with her, her first name is Candy. I thought, 'Wow, she's not sweet like candy!' I'm sure glad when I get to Chavez they'll be sophomores, and I won't have to deal with them."

"Have you guys ever called the school or anything?" Carmen asked.

"No," Jorge admitted.

"Well, thanks, Jorge and Elly," Ernesto said.

"No problem, man," Jorge responded, closing the door.

When Ernesto and Carmen returned to the Volvo, the girl's dark eyes were on fire. "That ugly Mrs. Serrano," Carmen fumed. "She hasn't got a clue what her little demon

121

is doing! Or maybe she does know, and she's in denial."

Ernesto kept quiet and drove. He figured he'd let Carmen release a little steam. She was quiet for a while and then spoke.

"It always amazes me when somebody commits some horrible crime. The parents come on the TV and say how good the kid was. They never expected something like this to happen, blah-blah. I bet when those criminals were kids, they were already doing horrible things. The parents were just looking the other way. The kids get worse and worse. By the time they're adults, they're monsters."

At midday on Wednesday, Penelope Ruiz went into Mrs. Sanchez's office. "Can I see you, please?" she asked. "This is really important."

"Of course, Penelope," Mrs. Sanchez responded. "It's Penelope *Ruiz*, right? Your brother Abel is a senior here."

"Yes, ma'am," Penelope replied. "I know you're busy, but this can't wait, you know?" She had several pieces of paper, stapled together and she put them on the principal's desk. "It's about bullying. It's really bad, Mrs. Sanchez."

"Bullying?" Mrs. Sanchez confirmed. The subject of bullying was in the news a lot lately. In a few extreme incidents around the country, children were bullied so badly that they turned violent. In other cases, bullied children killed themselves. Julia Sanchez was a compassionate principal, and, if bullying was a problem at Chavez, she wanted to know about it.

"Sit down, Penelope," Mrs. Sanchez said. "Just give me a minute, sweetheart, to make a quick call." She called Luis Sandoval and asked him to sub for her at a staff meeting she was due at in five minutes. "Thanks, Mr. Sandoval," she said on the phone. "An emergency has come up, and I must deal with it right away."

She closed the door to her office and sat down, facing Penelope, who was solemn-faced. "Penelope, what is this about?" she asked.

"Well," Penelope said, after taking a deep breath, "there are some girls in ninth grade—a couple boys too, but mostly girls. So, ever since school started, they've been doing awful stuff to other kids. But nobody'll say anything 'cause they don't want to be called a snitch. It's so bad that some kids don't even want to come to school anymore."

"Tell me what's going on, Penelope," Mrs. Sanchez urged her, a grieved look on her face.

"Well," Penelope continued, "the older kids, the eleventh- and twelfth-graders, they can tough it out. But the ninth-graders, some of them are just like little elementary school kids. Mrs. Sanchez, they're afraid anyway of coming to the big school. So they just put up with it. These bullies are steal-ing lunches. Sometimes, when a kid buys a piece of fruit at the vending machine, they steal that too. But that's not even the worst. The worst is what's happening to this girl. Her grandma has Parkinson's disease. Do you know what that disease is, Mrs. Sanchez?"

"Yes," Ms. Sanchez said, nodding. Sadness had come into her eyes, a deep sadness.

"Anyway, the girl has to take her grandmother for walks, or she'll get even worse. Her grandma walks funny, sorta stiff," Penelope went on. "The girl has to hold onto her grandmother so she doesn't fall down. These girls, they come over to her street, and they walk behind the girl and her grandma. They limp and act all weird, and they say they're zombies too."

Penelope said. "And they taunt the girl in school too. They say she's gonna get that sickness too and then she'll be a zombie. They wrote 'zombie' on her school binder. It's so bad the girl doesn't want to come to school anymore."

"Ohhh!" Mrs. Sanchez sighed. "How long has this been going on?"

"Like since school started," Penelope answered. "There's a lady who lives on the street—her son is a senior here. She sees the girls tormenting the girl and her grandma. She yelled at them to stop, but they laughed and called her a fat pig. Then they laughed and laughed."

Penelope dug into her backpack and pulled out a handful of paper-clipped sheets of paper. "I kinda asked some of the kids in ninth grade if they've been bullied since they came to school here. I asked them to sign their names if they'd been bullied, but they didn't want to sign their names. So they just put down their first initial and whether they were a boy or girl. Here's the list, Mrs. Sanchez."

The principal read through the sheets: A-boy . . . C-girl . . . A-girl . . . W-girl . . . M-boy . . .

There were fifty names.

Mrs. Sanchez felt sick. She felt worse than she had ever felt since becoming principal at Cesar Chavez High School. She was angry at herself for not detecting any of this. She spent so much time in meetings, here and downtown—faculty meetings and department meetings. She stared at the list of initials again, and she felt even sicker.

"Penelope, will you tell me the names of the girls who've been harassing the child and her grandmother?" Mrs. Sanchez asked.

Penelope withdrew another piece of paper from her jacket pocket. "Lacey Serrano and Candy Tellez are the girls who've been harassing Angel Roma. My middle school friend, Elly Aguilar, she's seen it. She wrote down here what she saw. Her mother made a note too. That's the lady the mean girls called a fat pig. Then Rocky Salcedo, he steals lunches. I put his name down too."

"Penelope, I promise you I will make what you have told me a top priority," Mrs. Sanchez vowed. "It took an amazing amount of courage for you to come in here and tell me this. I am so proud of you,

Penelope. You must have awesome parents. Did they encourage you to bring this to my attention for the sake of all the students at this school?"

"No," Penelope replied. "Actually, my mom told me not to do it. She said I'll just get in trouble, but I don't care. Mom said as long as I'm getting along, I shouldn't borrow trouble. 'MYOB,' she said. Dad agreed with her. Dad agrees with everything Mom says. But then I asked my big brother, Abel. He said to do it. He said little ninth-graders aren't tough enough to stand up for themselves. Somebody's gotta stand up for them. So I did it."

Mrs. Sanchez smiled. "Thank you, Penelope. Thank you more than I can say."

At the beginning of the following week, ninth-grade teachers and parent volunteers were much more in evidence during lunch and breaks. They didn't say anything. They just smiled at the students and kept a close eye on certain students they were told about. When Rocky Salcedo seemed to be muscling a smaller kid out of line, a teacher walked over to him. "Hi, Rocky," the teacher said. "My, what a big, strong boy you are. I bet you're good at sports. Part of being a good sport is keeping your place in line." Rocky looked shocked. The smaller boy got his lunch and walked away.

"You know what, Rocky?" the teacher continued, still smiling pleasantly. "A big boy like you is kinda scary to the ninth-graders. Some of them aren't as big as you yet. So we can depend on you to be aware of that, right?"

"Yeah, sure," Rocky Salcedo said.

That afternoon, Mrs. Sanchez called Lacey Serrano and Candy Tellez into her office. Lacey seemed especially nervous because she thought this was about the spray paint incident.

"Girls, you're both good students," Mrs. Sanchez began. "I see you're getting As and Bs in your classes. That's very good. I need for you to do a special project for the school. You want to help the school, right?"

"I didn't do that vandalism in the library," Lacey cried defensively. "I don't think it's right that I'm being punished for something I didn't do."

Mrs. Sanchez smiled. "Lacey, I couldn't agree with you more. Nobody should be punished for something they didn't do. And we haven't yet found out who vandalized the library. This is something else entirely."

Lacey fell silent, unsure of what Mrs. Sanchez was getting at. "What I want you girls to do," the principal went on, "is write a report on a medical issue. Do you remember how we talked about diabetes last month and how it can be prevented? We had a whole week on diet. Well, this is about a disease that attacks mostly older people, but sometimes it strikes younger people too. The project I want for you to do has to do with Parkinson's disease.

Both Lacey and Candy turned pale and frightened in their chairs. They looked at one another and seemed to shrink in size. Lacey scrunched down in her chair so far she looked like a much shorter girl. Candy glanced at Lacey in an angry way. It had originally been Lacey's idea to harass Angel Roma and her grandmother. Lacey said it would be fun.

"Do you know anybody with Parkinson's disease?" Mrs. Sanchez asked.

"No," Lacey almost screamed. "I never heard of it!"

"Me neither!" Candy said.

Ms. Sanchez said nothing. But she continued to stare at the girls as they squirmed in their chairs. At last, Lacey blurted, "If somebody told you some horrible lies about me and some lady on Finch Street, it's not true! I never even been on Finch Street."

"Me neither," Candy said.

"How come you know about an old lady with Parkinson's disease on Finch Street?" Mrs. Sanchez asked.

"*You* said it," Lacey stammered.

131

"No, I didn't, Lacey," Mrs. Sanchez replied. Her expression turned stern. "I am so very disappointed in you two ladies who attend our school. To think you would do something so cruel as to taunt a sick woman and her granddaughter."

"I didn't!" Lacey cried. "Angel Roma's lying!"

"Oh, Angel Roma didn't tell me," Mrs. Sanchez countered. "People who live on Finch Street were so sick at what they saw that *they* told me. I have testimony from people on Finch Street who saw you girls following the lady and her granddaughter. You were mimicking the woman's disability." Mrs. Sanchez waved some papers in the air. "Their statements are right here."

Lacey and Candy turned pale. Even their lips seemed to disappear.

"So, you are to work together to write a twenty-page report on Parkinson's disease," the principal commanded. "You may use books, magazines, the Internet. I want a thorough report on the symptoms, how the disease progresses, what treatments are effective, everything. I want you to pay particular attention to things that make the disease worse, like stress. I want this paper ten days from now."

"Ten days," Lacey wailed. "We can't do all that in ten days!"

"Twenty pages," Candy gasped. "I never wrote twenty pages on anything!"

"I'm sure you can do it," Mrs. Sanchez said. "I believe you girls have a lot of free time, or you wouldn't have been able to go all the way over to Finch Street so often." Mrs. Sanchez stood up and said, in an icy voice, "You can go now."

As Ernesto was leaving school that day, Richie Loranzo came over. His hands were stuffed in his pockets and he looked very worried. "Hi, Ernie," he said.

"Hi, Richie," Ernesto responded. "Something I can do for you?"

After the trip into the mountains, Richie was talking more and making friends with other kids. His teachers said he was even participating in class, which he had never done before. Ernesto was pleased at the progress the boy was making, but right now he seemed really upset.

"Can I talk to you, Ernie?" Richie asked.

"Sure, Richie. Come and sit in the Volvo. It's private there," Ernesto said.

Richie climbed into the passenger side of the front seat. He hung his head and chewed on his lip before he spoke. Then he said in a voice barely above a whisper. "I did it."

"What did you do, Richie?" Ernesto asked softly.

"I busted in the library, and I spray painted those words on the wall," Richie confessed. His lower lip was quivering.

Ernesto took a deep breath. "Why'd you do it, Richie?" he asked.

"'Cause I was mad. I hated school and stuff," Richie explained. "I was just mad at everybody, and I bought a can of spray paint and I did it."

"Why are you telling me now, Richie?" Ernesto asked.

"'Cause they're blaming that mean girl, Lacey Serrano," Richie answered. "She's gonna prove she didn't do it, and then they'll look for who really did it. They'll find me out anyway. I might as well tell before they come and find me."

Ernesto didn't sense any fear in the boy, just sadness. He didn't ask Ernesto what would happen to him when they found out. He probably didn't care. A boy who had suffered the trauma of what happened to his parents probably didn't care about anything.

"What do you want me to do about this, Richie?" Ernesto asked.

Richie looked at Ernesto with his big brown sad eyes. "I guess you'll have to tell the school," the boy said flatly. "And then they'll arrest me and put me in jail, but that's okay. I don't care."

"No, they won't put you in jail, Richie," Ernesto assured him. "You're only fourteen years old. Richie, how did you put the can of paint in Lacey's locker?"

"I don't remember," Richie mumbled.

"You used the spray paint on the library wall, Richie," Ernesto persisted. "But then the spray can was found in Lacey's locker. So how did that happen?"

"I . . . uh . . . wanted to get her in trouble because she's mean," Richie explained. "She hurts Angel Roma and her grandma all the time. Angel's so nice. I like her very much. She's the nicest girl I ever knew."

"Did you watch Lacey Serrano open her locker and keep track of the moves she made?" Ernesto asked. "Is that how you got the can in there?"

"Yeah, I guess that's what I did," Richie admitted.

Ernesto knew the boy was lying. The lie was written all over his tormented young face. But Ernesto had to be sure. "Richie," he asked, "I want to know why you chose red paint. Did that color mean something to you?"

"Yeah," Richie said. "I was so mad that I wanted to use red paint."

136

"Richie," Ernesto said softly, "red paint was not used in the vandalism."

Richie's eyes widened. "I meant the other paint. I got mixed up," he stammered. "What kinda paint was it?"

"Black paint," Ernesto answered.

"Yeah, yeah, now I remember. It was black paint," Richie said.

"Richie, you're not telling me the truth," Ernesto told him. "You're covering up for somebody."

Richie looked near tears. "I did it. I tell ya I did it. You gotta believe me, Ernie. If they don't believe I did it, then they'll blame Angel. I don't want them to blame Angel. That'd be awful. She's the nicest, sweetest girl I ever knew. I don't want nothing bad to happen to Angel."

"So you're confessing to something you didn't do to protect Angel, right?" Ernesto asked.

"Yeah," Richie admitted. "I gotta do this. Angel has that sick grandma and stuff. They put those mean pictures of her grandpa on line, and that made Angel cry. Angel's sorta my girlfriend, Ernie. You know what that is, don't you? A guy's gotta protect his girlfriend, right?" Richie's eyes welled with emotion. "Ain't that right, Ernie?"

"Richie," Ernesto suggested, "how about you and me going to Hortencia's and getting some tacos? Then I'll take you home."

"Okay," Richie said with a shrug.

"Richie, I don't want you to tell anybody what you just told me. Is that a deal?" Ernesto asked as he started the Volvo.

"Yeah, but I don't want Angel to get in trouble," Richie replied.

"Angel won't get in trouble, Richie, I promise you," Ernesto vowed. "But this is our secret. Don't you tell anybody what you told me. I'll take care of things, Richie. You're my little brother, *muchacho*. I'll make it okay. Trust me?"

CHAPTER EIGHT

After having tacos with Richie, Ernesto drove him home. Then he picked up Naomi, and they drove to Angel's house on Finch Street. Naomi had already met Angel's mother and grandmother, who was a sweet woman.

Ernesto and Naomi met with Angel's grandparents. Jesse Davila did most of the talking for them. Angel's mother was still at work. Angel was over at Penelope's house, and Abel was due to bring her home soon.

"Angel is a sweet and wonderful girl, and I'm so happy she's my little sister," Naomi told them. Ernesto had shared with Naomi what Richie told him, and they were both pretty sure about what had happened.

They had rehearsed how they would handle their meeting.

"Angel has a friend at school," Ernesto began. "He's in our program too. Richie Loranzo. He cares a lot for Angel."

"Yes," Mr. Davila replied. "I've met him. A nice boy."

Ernesto took a deep breath and then said, "Mr. Davila, this is difficult for me to tell you. I think that Angel might have spray painted the library a couple of weeks ago. Then she planted the paint can in Lacey Serrano's locker. Richie confessed to me that he did it, but I could tell he was lying. He was all mixed up about the details. And he kept saying, over and over, that he didn't want Angel to get in trouble. I think the kid was willing to take the blame to spare Angel."

"Oh my Lord!" Mr. Davila cried. "You know, the night it happened . . . one of my keys was missing, and Angel was gone from the house. She claimed she was going over to see Penelope. But when I called the Ruiz house, she wasn't there. She came home late, and she seemed very upset. I know Angel has been under a lot of stress—the bullying and all . . . I just didn't put her behavior together with the incident at school."

Mr. Davila put his hands over his face. His wife understood what Ernesto had said. In her slurred voice, she said, "The poor little thing . . . the poor little thing . . . "

When Abel dropped Angel home minutes later, the girl opened the door and stared at Ernesto and Naomi. Then she looked at her grandparents. She burst into tears. "You *know*," she sobbed. "Ohhh! I'm sorry, I'm sorry!"

"*Mi nieta*," Mr. Davila said in a sorrowful voice. "You spray painted the library. Then planted evidence on the mean girl to get her in trouble, didn't you?"

Angel stood rooted to the spot, tears running down her face. She was pale and trembling.

"Richie Loranzo told me he did it," Ernesto added. "He wanted to take the blame for you, Angel. He cares about you, but Richie is a very poor liar."

Naomi grabbed Angel and put her arms around her. "It's okay, sweetheart. We'll work something out."

Angel buried her face in Naomi's chest. "I'm sorry," the girl wept, her shoulders hunching with each sob. "It's just that . . . I was so mad . . . about stuff. I spray painted the library because they . . . those mean girls . . . were hurting me and Gram so bad. Nobody would do anything . . . and then . . . and then . . . I got an idea. I dug the spray can out from under my bed where I hid it. I watched Lacey open her locker, and then I knew how to do it. I stuck the can in there."

Angel's grandparents both hugged her, and she was in their arms as Ernesto and Naomi left. Mr. Davila said he would talk to Mrs. Sanchez and explain the situation in the morning.

Two days later, Mrs. Sanchez called Lacey Serrano into her office. "Lacey, we have solved the spray painting incident, and you are cleared. But I still expect that paper on Parkinson's disease from you and Candy," she advised curtly.

"Who did it?" Lacey demanded. "I got the right to know."

"You have no right to know anything, missy," Mrs. Sanchez told her. "And don't you dare talk to me in that tone of voice again. Some very fine seniors took up a collection to reimburse the school for what it cost to repaint the library wall. The matter is settled. And I expect that paper on time, or you'll be on detention for the rest of the year!"

Every day after school, for the next month, Angel Roma spent one hour helping the school librarian. They sorted books for an upcoming book fair at Cesar Chavez High School. It was said that Angel volunteered for the special project. Actually, she was atoning for her act of vandalism by what amounted to twenty-four hours of detention. But the only ones who knew that were Mrs. Sanchez, Angel's grandparents and mother, and Angel's special friends, Naomi and Ernesto.

The next Friday night, Ernesto took Naomi to the movies. As they drove to the theater, Ernesto was thinking about the kids in the big brother, big sister program. He said, "Naomi, do you know we've matched seventeen at-risk freshmen with seniors now? Mrs. Sanchez told me all kinds of creeps are targeting even middle school kids for gangs and drugs. The street gangs are especially looking ninth-graders to do their dirty work. They offer the kids money. But they also tell them that, because they're kids, even if they get caught, it won't go hard on them. Now these at-risk kids got a senior looking out for them."

"That's great, Ernie," Naomi responded. "That program was such a super idea."

"By the way, Naomi, the other day you said your mom was going in for a mammogram. Everything okay?" Ernesto knew that, when his mom checked in for one of those exams, everybody was a little nervous.

"Yeah, everything's fine, Ernie. Thanks for asking." Naomi reached over and put her hand on Ernesto's knee. "Mom had to go back because something looked unusual," she added. "But it turned out to be nothing. I was surprised at how upset Dad was."

Naomi seemed be cooking up an idea. "You know what, though?" she finally said. "Mom hasn't been out for a nice dinner for a while. And next Sunday, Dad's cousin, Monte Esposito, is having Dad and some other guys over for the big football game. Mom'll be home alone, and I thought I'd take her out to one of those nice Asian restaurants. She likes Asian food."

"Is that strictly a mother-daughter thing or . . . ?" Ernesto asked.

"Oh, Ernie, I'd love for you to come," Naomi replied, taking the cue right away. "You don't know how much Mom admires you. Once she said she wishes the Sandovals would adopt one of her boys. Then she could have you. She was just kidding, of course. She loves her boys, but they're a wild and woolly bunch sometimes. Do you like Japanese food?"

"Yeah, I do," Ernesto said emphatically. "I know a great place that serves awesome Asian food, the Sting Ray."

"Where Abel works?" Naomi asked.

"Yeah, he's been telling me about the Asian cuisine, and he's really into it," Ernesto answered. "Abel works there Sundays. He'd get a big kick out of making your mom's dinner. You know, the chefs often come out there and greet the guests, and Abel would be so proud."

"Sounds wonderful," Naomi said.

On Sunday, Ernesto drove over to the Martinez house and went inside. Brutus, the family pit bull, wagged his tail and greeted Ernesto like an old friend. When Felix Martinez first got Brutus, his wife had been terrified of the dog. She used to lock herself in the kitchen when the dog was loose. But over time Linda Martinez grew to love the dog as much as her husband did, maybe more. It turned out that Brutus was nothing like the stereotype of pit bulls. He was a lovable clown.

"So, Mrs. Martinez," Ernesto remarked, "your husband is over watching the big game."

"Yes, his cousin has one of these giant screens," Mrs. Martinez replied. "When those big guys come running with the football it seems like they're in your face! I don't like football anyway. I don't like any sports, except maybe figure skating. Do you like football, Ernie?"

"It's okay," Ernesto responded. "I'll watch if I like the team or the quarterback or if some local guys got a shot. I'm not that much into baseball or football. I love to run on the track team. That's fun. And it's something I can do on my own when I'm done with school."

Naomi giggled. "Remember how upset Dad was when he found out you didn't like football? He thought every real man ought to love football."

"Yeah," Ernesto laughed too. "He thought I was a wimp."

As they all went outside, Linda Martinez smiled and commented, "Oh, you still have your Volvo. They're such safe, reliable cars."

Ernesto gave Naomi a look and growled under his breath, "Dear old Viola!"

Naomi was giggling when she got into the car.

When they were seated at the Sting Ray with their menus, Mrs. Martinez was so happy. "Oh, this is such a treat. I love Asian food, and Felix hates it, so we never have it at home." She ordered Thai chicken with basil over rice with chopped peanuts and shredded coconut. Ernesto and Naomi went for the spicy pork ribs brushed with orange marmalade.

As they waited for their entrees to be served, Mrs. Martinez confided, "You

148

know, I dearly love Felix, and he's a good man. There's no doubt about that. All during our marriage, he's worked hard and taken care of me and his kids. I never knew a man to work harder"

Mom sighed. "But he has this hot temper, and sometimes I'm so hurt by what he says. I should be used to it by now. He doesn't mean to hurt me, I'm sure. But when he yells and criticizes me, I just sort of curl up inside and ache."

Naomi glanced at Ernesto. A slow current of sadness flowed through Naomi's eyes.

Her mother continued. "You hear so much about this domestic abuse, and Felix doesn't do that. I mean, years ago there was some pushing and shoving, but nothing serious. I can't complain about that. But the words, they can hurt too. They don't leave scars you can see, but I think they do leave scars . . . you know, inside."

Mrs. Martinez ran her finger down the water glass, leaving a line in the moisture on its side. As she spoke again, her gaze was on the glass. "My own father was the same way. A good, hardworking man, but he could be cruel to my mother. I would see her crying. I guess I thought that's the way things were. That it's something a woman just has to put up with. You had to be grateful if your husband was faithful, and my father was. My father never looked at another woman, and your father, Naomi, he's always been faithful. And that's a blessing."

She lifted her head and looked right at Naomi. "You know, I always wanted a girl, but then Orlando and Manny came. Then Zack. And I thought maybe that was best. If there was a girl, she'd have to go through so much. And then, Naomi, you came along, and I was so happy. But then when you got older and started dating Clay Aguirre, my heart just ached."

"Yeah," Naomi agreed ruefully. "I put up with a lot from that jerk."

"He'd come to pick you up and sit in his car honking his horn," Mrs. Martinez remarked. "I'd hear him yelling for you to hurry up. *I felt so bad for you.*"

The woman's face lit up then. "And then you came along, Ernie. Oh, it was so wonderful. When you'd come to pick up Naomi, you'd come in the house and talk to us, to Felix and me. You were nice and polite. You don't know how many times I said to myself *gracias a Dios*!"

Ernesto felt genuinely touched by the woman's words. "That's very kind of you to say, Mrs. Martinez," he told the mother. "I love Naomi very much, and I think she has a great mom."

The meal was delivered, and it was perfect. Mrs. Martinez kept raving over how good everything was. "I love Mexican food, of course," she commented, "but it's so nice to have a change."

As they were finishing their meal, Abel Ruiz appeared at their table. "Was everything all right?" he asked, smiling. He looked much older than he did at school, in his starched white blouse and apron with the Sting Ray logo.

"It's all wonderful, Abel," Mrs. Martinez replied. "Such a marvelous meal."

"Yes, Abel," Naomi added. "I've never tasted such delicious pork."

"Another home run, dude," Ernesto said.

At that moment, a pretty girl appeared, her long dark hair tied up in a bun. She was also wearing a starched white blouse and apron. Abel made the introductions. "This is Cassie Ursillo. Her uncle is the big honcho around here."

Cassie smiled and said, "Doesn't Abel have James Dean eyes?"

Abel laughed. "Most people don't even know who the dude was. He died like a hundred years ago."

"Oh no," Mrs. Martinez corrected him. "My mother just loved him. When I was a little girl, I saw his old movies on television. Something about a rebel. I was sad when I found out he was dead. And, yes, Abel *does* have those dreamy eyes."

Cassie slipped her hand under Abel's arm. "Time to go back to the kitchen, chef."

When Abel and Cassie were gone, Ernesto declared, "She'd like to hook Abel, but he's not buying. . . . Okay, who's for dessert?"

Later, as they headed home, Mrs. Martinez remarked, "This has been such a lovely day. I'm so happy you came, Ernie. It made it extra special."

"Thank you. I enjoyed it too," Ernesto responded.

Naomi turned on the radio and tuned to the game. They all listened in silence for a few minutes. "Uh-oh!" Naomi groaned. "The Chargers are losing."

"Felix'll be in a bad mood when he gets home," Mrs. Martinez sighed.

"They're down just one touchdown . . . they've been known to bring it home at the last minute," Ernesto said.

"Every time they lose, Felix curses the coach and yells about firing him," Mrs. Martinez explained.

As Ernesto pulled onto the freeway, a car sped past, going very fast. Few motorists kept to the seventy-mile-per-hour limit, but this car seemed to be going ninety or better.

"Look!" Naomi noted in a suddenly frightened voice. "He's changing lanes like crazy. I thought he'd rear-end that van."

The car was a silver Infiniti built for speed. Ernesto didn't know anybody who owned one except his AP History teacher, Mr. Bustos. Of course, Ernesto thought, there had to be a lot of other Infinitis on the road.

"He's changed lanes again," Naomi gasped.

"Oh my gosh!" Mrs. Martinez cried. "He almost sideswiped that truck."

"Call nine-one-one, Naomi," Ernesto directed. "Tell them there's a dangerous driver out here. Could be drunk."

Naomi pulled out her cell phone. "We're southbound on the six-oh-five, nearing the Washington Street off ramp," she told the 911 dispatcher. "There's a silver Infiniti driving really crazy. I think he's hit a hundred miles per hour. Oh no! That truck swerved to miss him. It's in a spin!"

Mrs. Martinez clasped her hands to her cheeks. A Toyota pickup truck had gotten hit by the swerving bigger truck, and the van behind them couldn't stop and plowed into them. Three vehicles were in a tangled wreck, but the Infiniti was out of sight.

"Oh, there's been a horrible accident," Naomi almost screamed into her phone. "Please send help right away!"

Ernesto pulled the Volvo to the shoulder of the road and out of the freeway lane, at a safe distance from the accident. Two other motorists who'd witnessed what happened also stopped. Police sirens and emergency vehicles wails filled the late afternoon.

"We've got to tell the police what caused that accident," Ernesto said. His heart was pounding as a highway patrolman came walking up.

"Officer," Ernesto told him, "a silver Infiniti was driving really crazy, weaving in and outta lanes. He swerved into the lane that the big Ford pickup was in, and the Ford swerved into the blue Toyota. The van just couldn't stop fast enough. The guy in the Infiniti caused the whole thing. You gotta find him. He could do it all again."

The highway patrol office called in the information right away. He then took Ernesto's statement and the statements of the other drivers. Nobody had been able to get a license number on the Infiniti. All Ernesto hoped was that the creep driving the Infiniti hadn't gotten clean away.

Ernesto continued the drive home, caught up in the massive snarl of traffic. Two lanes of traffic were shut down by the wreckage and emergency vehicles. Traffic inched past the scene. The motorists slowing down for a look made matters even worse.

As Ernesto was finally exiting the freeway, he saw a medical helicopter overhead. "Oh man. Somebody hurt bad," he remarked. "I bet that Infiniti driver was drunk. You don't drive like that unless you're dead drunk!"

CHAPTER NINE

When Ernesto dropped Naomi and her mother home, Mr. Martinez was already there. "The lousy bums fumbled the ball," he was ranting. "They coulda got a touchdown, but that lousy butterfingers fumbled the ball. What kinda idiots are they draftin'? Pop Warner kids do better. Can't even hold onta the football! I'd fire the bum out tonight. Let him drive a garbage truck."

"Felix," Linda Martinez told him, "there was a terrible accident on the freeway. We saw it happen."

"Ah, so what?" Mr. Martinez stormed. "I had a hundred dollar bet goin' on this stinkin' game. I don't care about some stupid fender bender on the freeway. What are you talkin' about that for? Like I care."

The familiar look of hurt passed through Linda Martinez's eyes.

"Daddy," Naomi said sharply, "the medical helicopter was called. Somebody was badly hurt. It was right at the Washington off ramp."

Ernesto chimed in. "Some jerk driving an Infiniti was going a hundred miles an hour, and he forced a Ford truck into a Toyota and then another van piled on."

"Well then," Mr. Martinez sneered, "I hope the Infiniti cracked up too. Lousy rich bums think they can get away with murder. Like those football players. Make a coupla million bucks a year, and they can't play worth spit. You think they make them give back their millions when they fumble the ball? I make a mistake on the forklift, and I gotta worry about my job."

"Felix," Linda Martinez said softly, "we had such a nice dinner. We went to the Sting Ray and—"

"What's that got to do with anything?" Mr. Martinez barked. "Listen to her. She's talking about dinner when I lost a big bet on that lousy football game."

Naomi looked embarrassed for her father. She forced a smile to her lips and turned to Ernesto. "See you tomorrow, Ernie, and thanks for coming."

"Yes, Ernie," Linda Martinez added. "It was lovely." She turned and hurried to her room to change out of her dress-up clothes.

"Uh, Naomi, want to take a walk or something?" Ernesto asked. He hated to leave with Felix Martinez in such a bad mood.

"I'd love to, Ernie, but I promised Mom I'd help her measure the new drapes she's making," Naomi replied. Then, when her father went into the kitchen, Naomi explained. "I don't want to leave Mom with him ranting. Now that Zack doesn't live here anymore . . . when it's just the two of them, he can get . . . you know . . . "

Naomi had three older brothers. Orlando and Manny worked in a Latin band in Los

Angeles. Zack had worked with his father in construction until they had a bitter falling out. Now Zack was in Los Angeles too, working as a gofer with the band. Felix Martinez's bad temper had driven all three boys out of the house. The boys visited and were in touch, but they couldn't live under the same roof as their father.

"I understand," Ernesto said. He kissed Naomi and went out to his Volvo.

It had been a pleasant day until they got back to the Martinez house. Ernesto genuinely liked Felix Martinez. He *was* a decent man, but his rages upset Ernesto. When Ernesto first met Mr. Martinez, he disliked him. He seemed like an ogre. But little by little, Ernesto saw his good side. In fact, Ernesto was instrumental in bringing about a reconciliation between Felix Martinez and two of his sons, Orlando and Manny. After a huge family fight, they had not spoken to each other in years.

As much as Felix Martinez's outbursts bothered Ernesto, he was still the father of the girl Ernesto dearly loved. Naomi was part of Felix Martinez, and Ernesto had to accept it. Naomi loved her father in spite of everything, so Ernesto accepted him too.

Ernesto sadly recalled what Linda Martinez had said in the Sting Ray. Cruel words leave scars too. Felix Martinez's words had left a few more scars today.

A ranting Mr. Martinez was one thing. But, in the back of Ernesto's mind, he had a nagging fear about the Infiniti that had caused the terrible accident. Was it connected to Quino Bustos, his teacher? That couldn't be, Ernesto told himself.

When Ernesto got home, his mother greeted him at the door. "Oh, Ernie, I'm so glad to see you," she told him. "I heard about that terrible accident on the freeway, and I thought you were probably on it at that time. I tried to call you on your cell phone, but I kept being shifted to voice mail."

"I'm sorry, Mom," Ernesto apologized. "I forgot to turn my phone on. We saw the accident happen. This silver Infiniti was speeding and changing lanes, and who-ever was driving it caused the whole acci-dent. They forced a big truck into a smaller Toyota pickup. It was coming right up the Washington on ramp. They took somebody away in a medical chopper."

"Somebody's in critical condition," Maria Sandoval said. "It just came over the radio."

At that moment, Luis Sandoval pulled into the driveway. When he came through the doorway, he had a terrible look on his face.

"Dad, we saw this horrible accident on the freeway," Ernesto started to say. "Dad . . . what's the matter?"

"Sal Ruiz," Ernesto's father responded. "Abel's dad . . . he was in that accident. He's in bad shape at the hospital. I just got a call from Abel. He tried to call you, but you weren't answering."

Ernesto went numb. Finally, he gasped, "What hospital?"

"Mercy," Dad replied.

"Luis," Maria Sandoval said, "we've got to be there for Liza and Penelope."

"Mama will stay with the girls and Alfredo," Luis Sandoval directed. "We'll go in the minivan."

As Ernesto got into the minivan, he called Naomi. "Did you hear—" he started to say.

"We're on our way to Mercy," Naomi interrupted. She sounded as if she'd been crying.

When the Sandovals arrived at Mercy, they went to the emergency waiting room. Felix, Linda, and Naomi Martinez were already there. Emilio, Conchita, and Carmen Ibarra arrived just after the Sandovals. In the corner of the room, Liza Ruiz and Penelope sat huddled, their eyes reddened. They clung to each other like survivors of a disaster. Abel sat alone, staring ahead, rigid in shock. When Paul and David Morales arrived, they both went to Abel, hugging him.

"He's in surgery," Liza Ruiz told them between sobs. "The nice young doctor came to see us. He said he'd come here when it's over and . . . and . . . tell us."

Suddenly Penelope erupted. "It's not fair!" she cried. "Poor Daddy. He never gets any breaks. It wasn't his fault. That freakin' Infiniti pushed the truck into him. He didn't have a chance. Poor Daddy. He takes lousy overtime on Sunday to fix some freakin' rich man's retaining wall. Why can't he rest on Sunday? Even God said to do that. But he has to work, like a slave— and on Sunday—just to make a few more lousy bucks."

Mrs. Ruiz was too worried to say anything to her daughter.

Abel was slumped in his chair, his head down. Paul knelt beside him, his hand on Abel's shoulder. Ernesto walked over and grabbed Abel's hand. "It's gonna be okay, *mi amigo*," Ernesto assured his friend.

Abel looked up, his dark eyes wet from crying. "No, it's not," he cried. "Like Penny says . . . he never gets any breaks. He's gonna die. He never had any luck.

My father never had nothin'. It's all down-hill for him. Now he's gonna die, his head smashed in a stinkin' accident. I was gonna make money as a chef. I was gonna take care of him so that he wouldn't have to work when his back was killing him. And now . . . now I don't get the chance 'cause he's not gonna make it, Ernie."

Ernesto knelt on the floor on the other side of where Paul was. He held tightly to Abel's hand. "Listen to me, homie. Your dad's gonna be okay. He's a strong man. He's one of the strongest men I ever saw. He's gonna fight his way through this. He's gonna grin at you and say *'mi hijo*, I'm back.'"

Abel sobbed against Ernesto's chest for a few minutes.

Felix Martinez stood with his wife and daughter, his face grim. "When they find the guy who was driving that Infiniti, he oughta be strung up in the *barrio*. He hadda be a drunk. I could take the guy out myself, I'm telling you."

166

"I'm with you, dude," Paul Morales agreed. "You put the noose around his neck, and I'll kick the box from under his feet."

David Morales drew close to Abel. "Abel," he said in almost a whisper, "it's not necessarily so bad. When I was in prison, there was a terrible fight between two guys. One guy whacked the other with a cement block upside his head, and they thought he was a goner. But the doctors saved him. The doctors can do amazing things with head injuries. You gotta have faith, Abel. All the prayers and all the love in this room for your dad, it's gonna work, man."

Paul Morales was standing now, a dark look on his face. Ernesto looked at him and thought he was just like Felix Martinez right now, gripped by hatred.

When the young doctor came into the room, everyone seemed to stop breathing. He was in scrubs, with a surgical cap on and a mask unfastened at his neck. There was no sound at all. The doctor's eyes searched the crowd of people until they settled on Liza Ruiz.

"Mrs. Ruiz," he said in a tentative voice.

"Yes," Liza Ruiz answered in a faint voice. Maria Sandoval and Conchita Ibarra stood on either side of her, supporting her with their arms. Linda Martinez held her hand.

"Your husband came through the surgery, Mrs. Ruiz," the doctor told her. "He's still in very critical condition in the recovery room. He'll be moved to the ICU in about an hour. It's much too early to make a prognosis, but it's encouraging that he survived the surgery. At this point, we are hopeful."

"When can I see my husband?" Liza Ruiz asked in a trembling voice.

"In about an hour," the surgeon replied, placing his hand on Mrs. Ruiz's for a moment. "The ICU nurse will be in touch with you."

When they were allowed to see Sal Ruiz, he was, of course, still sedated and connected to many tubes and monitors. But he was alive, and that was all his friends and family needed for the moment. The priest from Our Lady of Guadalupe Church came to the ICU to administer the holy anointing. "Through this holy anointing," he intoned, "may the Lord in His love and mercy help you with the grace of the Holy Spirit."

Ernesto and Paul and David Morales remained with Liza Ruiz in the ICU waiting room through most of the night. Naomi and her mother, Maria Sandoval, and Conchita Ibarra remained too. Liza Ruiz wanted to send Penelope home with Luis Sandoval, but the girl would not leave. Luis Sandoval, Felix Martinez, and Emilio Ibarra promised to return early in the morning to take their family members home.

In the quiet of the middle of the night, the atmosphere of despair had lifted somewhat. Friends were sitting around Liza Ruiz and Penelope when a young man stepped into the room. His hair was uncombed, and his clothing looked as though he'd thrown on anything at hand.

"Tomás!" Liza Ruiz screamed. "Oh, Tomás! Your father was hurt so badly. His head . . . oh . . . and he has broken bones, but there is hope."

"I came the minute I got your message, Mom," Tomás cried. He embraced his mother and rocked her gently for what seemed an eternity.

In the very early morning, the surgeon came back to the ICU waiting room to talk to the family. He'd examined Sal Ruiz, and he was holding his own. There was no way to tell yet when he could be upgraded from critical to serious. Complications were still possible, but the outlook was brighter than they were the night before. He didn't yet know whether Sal Ruiz had suffered any permanent damage.

"Maria," Liza Ruiz directed, "take Penelope home when Luis comes. Abel and I will stay here a while longer." Penelope finally agreed to go with Ernesto's mother, and Conchita Ibarra also went home. Like Maria Sandoval, she had young children at home to take care of.

Ernesto, Naomi, and Paul Morales remained with the Ruiz family.

"You've got to eat some breakfast, Mom," Tomás advised. "You look like you're going to collapse."

"I can't," Liza Ruiz objected. "I couldn't get anything down my throat. Not until I talk to Sal and know he's going to be all right."

"That'll take time, Mom," Abel said.

"Come on, Mrs. Ruiz," Ernesto suggested gently. "We'll all go down to the cafeteria here and get you some eggs and coffee. You can down that. You need to be strong for when your husband gets out of here and recovers at home."

"Just some nice eggs and maybe a little toast," Naomi urged, gently tugging on Liza Ruiz's arm.

"Come on, Mom," Abel said. "If you conk out on us, where're we gonna be?

You're the strong one, Mom. It's always been that way. Pop's countin' on ya."

Finally Liza Ruiz stood, and the six of them rode the elevator to the hospital cafeteria.

As she picked at her eggs and toast, Mrs. Ruiz remarked, "We have auto insurance and medical. And, thank God, Sal's covered for medical expenses. I hope it's all covered."

"Don't worry about that, Mrs. Ruiz," Paul Morales growled, a fierce sneer on his lips. "We'll get the dude who drove the Infiniti, and you can sue that sucker to his last drop of blood." The rage deepened in Paul's face. "Must be a rich creep to own a car like that. Get a really vicious lawyer."

Abel's phone rang. It was Penelope. She'd already called Abel on his cell phone five times, and it wasn't even six in the morning yet. Abel assured her that their father was holding his own. Abel and Penelope would skip classes at Cesar Chavez High today, but Ernesto and Naomi decided to go. They

172

were both in need of a shower, but that would come when they got home from school later in the day. Both of Mrs. Ruiz's sons were with her to support her. She urged everybody to leave, including Paul and David Morales, who had jobs to go to.

Luis Sandoval swung by the hospital to pick up Ernesto and Naomi, and they headed for Chavez High.

As the drove to the school, Ernesto brought up what was on his mind. "You know, Dad, Quino Bustos, my AP History teacher, he drives a silver Infiniti."

"Ah yes, Mr. Bustos always parks that car of his in the same spot in the faculty parking lot," Dad commented. "He uses a corner place where his beloved Infiniti is least likely to be dinged. I always put my minivan right beside him."

"I'm sure the maniac driving on the freeway yesterday wasn't him," Ernesto responded, "but it's just weird. The last anybody saw of the Infiniti after the accident, it was going down the Washington Street ramp."

"The guy in the Infiniti caused the accident, but he didn't hit anybody," Naomi noted. "How are they going to prove a case against him if his car isn't damaged?"

Luis Sandoval said, "We may have gotten lucky. I heard that the car clipped a dump truck going off the Washington Street ramp. I'm not sure, but that's the rumor."

"Oh, wow! I hope so," Naomi cried. "To bring so much misery to poor Mr. Ruiz and his family."

Luis Sandoval was approaching his regular parking spot.

"Look, Dad," Ernesto gasped. "No Infiniti!" A numbness crept through his body. He saw a brief flash of concern on his father's face. Mr. Bustos was a brilliant and respected teacher. Surely he couldn't have been driving so recklessly yesterday, scattering cars like toys. It didn't make sense. Ernesto got out of the Cavalier as a beige Honda drove into the faculty lot and eased into Mr. Bustos's usual spot.

Mr. Bustos got out of the Honda, carrying his very fine briefcase from the brand designer Santiago Gonzalez. The briefcase must have cost close to a thousand dollars. Luis Sandoval had purchased his briefcase for thirty dollars at the outlet store.

Mr. Bustos nodded a good-morning to everyone and strode toward his classroom with his usual energy. He always seemed to be delighted to be teaching. He gave the impression that there was nothing in the world he'd rather be doing. That was one of the reasons that most of his students, including Ernesto, liked him. The guy loved to teach, and his enthusiasm came on as exciting.

Mr. Bustos could *not* have been driving the Infiniti yesterday, Ernesto told himself. He was a good, honorable man. If he had caused that nightmare on the freeway yesterday, he would not be cheerfully heading for his classroom. He could not be so eager, as usual, to share his knowledge. It was just a coincidence that a silver Infiniti, like the one Mr. Bustos owned, had been involved in the tragic accident, Ernesto decided.

Ernesto followed Mr. Bustos into the classroom and sat in his usual place. Mr. Bustos looked up at Ernesto, and Ernesto's legs grew weak. Ernesto saw something in the man's eyes that he had never seen before. Maybe, Ernesto thought, his imagination was at work, but Mr. Bustos did not look right.

During class, the man was off his stride. Everyone noticed it. He seemed uninvolved in the class discussions, and, for the last twenty minutes of the class, he assigned the students to use their laptops to research recent developments in the Arab world. He said that the Arab countries were reaching for democracy. Some of their leaders, he explained, were consulting early American constitutional government to help them draft their own constitutions.

CHAPTER TEN

The minute Ernesto left class, he got a call from Paul Morales. "Hey, Ernesto. Paul here," he said. "I stopped by Mercy to check on Mr. Ruiz. He's still critical but stable. It's a good sign. Me and Mrs. Ruiz's boys convinced the poor lady to go home and get some rest. You must be beat too, dude. You didn't get any sleep last night."

"I'm okay, man," Ernesto replied. He wanted to tell Paul about Quino Bustos's Infiniti being missing. Before he could, Paul told him, "Dude, I got some news about the accident. That silver Infiniti hit a dump truck after causing the accident. Back fender was pretty badly crumpled.

You know what that means, homie? Maybe we got a hook into that scum!"

"That's a break, Paul," Ernesto responded.

"The cops got no license number," Paul added. "So what they're gonna have to do is wait for a silver Infiniti to show up at the autobody shop. The scum'll probably sneak it down to Mexico and get the work done there. And he'll get a paint job so it won't be silver no more."

"Dude," Ernesto said, "you know, my AP History teacher has a silver Infiniti. I mean, no way in the world could he have been driving that car yesterday. He's a good, solid guy, but maybe he loaned the car to somebody or . . ."

"He come to class this morning?" Paul asked suspiciously.

"Yeah, driving a different car, a Honda. A rental," Ernesto answered. Ernesto was nervous about sharing all this with Paul. Paul could be a loose cannon. He was filled with rage over the accident to start

178

with. His close friend Abel had his father hanging between life and death in the hospital, all because of some dude in a silver Infiniti.

"Oh man!" Paul growled. "Do you know where this dude Bustos lives?"

"Listen, Paul," Ernesto said coolly, "you're gonna keep a cool head about this, aren't you? I don't want you going off half cocked and getting yourself in trouble."

"Don't worry. I'm cool. Where does he live?" Paul assured him.

"When I first started going to that class, Mr. Bustos invited us all over to his house," Ernesto explained. "It's not in the heart of the *barrio*, but it's off Washington, up in the hills where they got some nice houses. You can see the bay from the house. It's kinda old, but elegant. It's right on Luther Burbank Lane. It's the first house on the street, green, with a red roof."

"Got it," Paul responded. "Okay, homie, me and Cruz'll look around. Maybe the Infiniti is sitting there in the driveway with a bashed in fender, or maybe it's locked in the garage. That's okay. Cruz's good at—"

"Paul, *please*, man," Ernesto pleaded, "I'd never forgive myself if you got in trouble over something I told you. Cruz too. You guys are my friends. Don't do anything illegal, okay?"

"Dude, you crazy? Me and Cruz do something illegal?" Paul's tone did little to reassure Ernesto, as he ended the call.

At noon, Ernesto got another call from Paul. "Garage was empty, man," Paul reported. "No Infiniti. But me and Cruz got some info, though. The dude's got a son, a guy about twenty-five, a real piece of work. He hangs out at the Cat's Paw on Polk with some low-life friends. His daddy's divorced, inherited a fortune from his folks. So the chicks think this guy Basil's a good catch."

"So what?" Ernesto was thinking. Then Paul said something that started ringing a bell. "The son's name's Basilio, but he calls himself Basil. He likes to go slummin'. He's got two DUIs already. Some slimy lawyer, one of those who advertise on the radio that they'll get you off DUIs, got the kid cleaned up. Basil's the apple of his father's eye. Started as a freshman at Yale, dropped out, switched to another Ivy League school. Then he got bounced outta there for wild frat parties, where some chicks made charges. Ernie, the apple of pop's eye is rotten and fulla worms. I'll give you ten to one he was at the wheel."

"Oh brother!" Ernesto groaned.

"Little punk is probably in Mexico right now getting the car fixed," Paul continued. "Probably it'll come back candy apple red. And he's gonna get away with almost killin' Abel's father and banging up all those other people. Three people, besides Mr. Ruiz, in the hospital with broken bones."

"What can we do, Paul?" Ernesto asked.

"I don't know about you, homie, but that rat almost put my buddy's pop in the ground. He ain't gonna run free," Paul swore. "Sooner or later, this Basil Bustos is gonna be driving a red Infiniti back to the *barrio* with a shiny new fender. Whenever he shows his face, he's gonna have a real unfriendly reception committee."

Ernesto ended the call with a lot of mixed feelings. He hoped Paul wouldn't do something foolish and get himself into trouble. He felt uneasy about the information he now had. Should he call the police? Ernesto also felt sorry for Mr. Bustos. If his son was driving the car that caused that terrible accident, Mr. Bustos must be devastated. But Paul Morales was right. Basil Bustos could not be allowed to get away with this. He caused an accident that hurt a lot of people, one critically. And he fled the scene.

Ernesto called Abel. "You still at the hospital?"

"Yeah, we brought Mom back," Abel responded. "She took a nap at home, but she insisted on being here again. Dad's doin' pretty good. He even opened his eyes and tried to smile, but his mouth is all banged up. Doctor said he's stayin' in the ICU a couple more days. Then he'll be moved to a regular room if there aren't any complications."

"Does he even know what happened?" Ernesto asked.

"No, man," Abel answered. "We think he was tryin' to say 'What happened,' but we're not sure. I whispered a little in his ear about the accident. I think he got it."

"We're all praying and rooting for him, man," Ernesto assured Abel. He didn't want to mention his and Paul's suspicions about Mr. Bustos's son. Not yet.

After Luis Sandoval and Ernesto got home, they took a walk. Ernesto needed to talk to his dad, and talking always seemed easier on one of their walks.

"How well do you know Quino Bustos, Dad?" Ernesto asked.

"Not very well, but he's always nice when we talk," Dad replied. "We get along well at the history department meetings. Why?"

"Dad, you remember—I mentioned it before—the silver Infiniti," Ernesto said.

"Yes, Mr. Bustos has one just like the guy who caused the accident yesterday, but surely—" A look of shock came over Luis Sandoval's face. "Ernesto, I can't believe you'd think Mr. Bustos was in any way involved! A criminal driving the Infiniti caused the accident, not a respectable man like Mr. Bustos. It has to be a coincidence, an awful coincidence."

"Dad, Mr. Bustos has a son named Basil," Ernesto explained. "He's already got two DUIs. I mean, Mr. Bustos could've loaned the car to his son. Mr. Bustos seemed distracted in class today."

Dad grasped his brow and cried, "*Por Dios*! I can't believe Mr. Bustos knows that his son did such a thing and is covering it up."

"Paul Morales is really steamed," Ernesto went on. "He loves Abel. He checked out the Bustos home. No sign of the Infiniti. And you were right. The Infiniti sideswiped a truck and got some damage on the back fender. Paul checked the garage too, but no luck."

CHAPTER TEN

"Paul broke into the garage?" Dad asked, his eyebrows going up.

"Well, he didn't admit to that," Ernesto replied.

"Ernie, you tell that boy he's going to end up in worse trouble than his brother if he's not careful," Dad commanded. "I like Paul Morales. He's a very decent young man with a lot of potential. I don't want anything bad to happen to him."

Father and son walked a short while. Then Luis Sandoval spoke. "What you've got here, Ernie, is what your Uncle Arturo would call circumstantial evidence. For all we know, the Infiniti Mr. Bustos drives is in the garage for an oil change."

"Yeah," Ernesto admitted, "but Paul is afraid the busted car is in Mexico getting a major face lift. When it reappears, the dude'll be scot free. He almost killed Abel's dad. That isn't right. Basil Bustos has a record of drunk driving, and slimy lawyers have helped him beat the rap. Next time he might kill a whole family."

"Tell you what, Ernie," Mr. Sandoval said. "Let's be up front with Quino. I'm going over to his house and tell him what's going on. I'm not going to accuse him or his son. I'll tell him there are rumors, and he needs to deal with them. I'd like for you to come too, Ernie. We're not going to come on as accusatory, just as concerned friends. If, God forbid, it was his Infiniti on Sunday and if his son was at the wheel, he may not even know what happened. Maybe the kid lied to him."

"Okay, Dad. I'm with you," Ernesto agreed. He was ashamed, though, of what was going through his mind. Ernesto desperately wanted a good grade and college credit in that AP History class. If Mr. Bustos took this visit the wrong way—as an attack on him and his son—who knows what might happen? Who could prove whether Ernesto's lowered grade was an act of retaliation or just a coincidence?

But Ernesto knew it had to be done.

About twenty minutes later, the Sandovals turned up toward the hills. They came to a stop at a large, ornate house on Luther Burbank Lane. The garage door was open, and the Honda rental was parked inside.

Mr. Bustos happened to be standing outside when the Sandovals arrived. He came walking over to the minivan. "Well, hi, Luis. Hi, Ernesto. What brings you to my place?" He smiled and remarked, "Quite a view, eh?"

"Beautiful," Luis Sandoval responded. "Quino, I'm sure you heard about the terrible accident yesterday near the Washington Street ramp."

"Ah yes, one of our students almost lost his father," Mr. Bustos answered. "I hope the man is doing better." Once more, maybe Ernesto's imagination was at work, but he thought he saw a strange look on Mr. Bustos's face.

"Yes, he is. We're all hoping and expecting him to make a full recovery."

"That's good," Mr. Bustos responded.

"Quino," Luis Sandoval began, "I just wanted to give you a heads-up on some rumors floating around the school. Ernie here has heard them. You probably heard that the accident was caused by a speeding silver Infiniti. Of course, nobody thinks you were driving it. But some of the kids are saying you might have loaned the car to your son and—"

"Ah!" Mr. Bustos interrupted, shaking his head. "And this morning my Infiniti is missing, and they've put the pieces together. This has fueled the fires of gossip, I'm sure."

The man turned to address Ernesto. "Well, Ernie, you're senior class president, and your word has a lot of gravitas. So I'm depending on you to set the record straight and end any ridiculous rumors. The Infiniti that caused that dreadful tragedy on the freeway was not mine. I did, in fact, loan my Infiniti to my son on Saturday night. And he left on Saturday night. He's driving the car to Brandeis University where he's going to become a student. Basil has texted me several times that the road trip is going very well. So, you see, by the time of that accident, my son and the Infiniti were going somewhere through Arizona. The scoundrel who caused the accident is someone else."

"Well, I'm glad we talked, Quino," Luis responded. "Unless we put a stop to rumors like this quickly, they just keep growing."

"Yes indeed," Mr. Bustos agreed. "Mystery solved." He turned again to Ernesto. "So do your best to quell all this nonsense, Ernesto. Tell your friends at school that my Infiniti is going to be soon driving up to Brandeis University."

Ernesto nodded. "Yes, sir," he told the man. But his mouth was very dry. His heart was beating rapidly. He felt sick. Mr. Bustos put on a good front, but his explanation had holes in it. Holes big enough to drive an Infiniti through.

Father and son exchanged good-byes with Mr. Bustos and got back into the minivan. Leaving the Bustos home, Ernesto asked, "Well, Dad, what do you think?"

Luis Sandoval shook his head. "Oh man, Ernie, something bad is going down. I've never seen such a look on Quino's face. He's not totally clueless, that's for sure. The story about the boy driving across the country to Brandeis in his father's luxury car . . . "

Ernesto's cell rang. "Ernie, this is Paul." Paul Morales was speaking in a tense voice. "Me and Cruz and Beto are over here at the Cat's Paw on Polk Street. The punk's in here drinkin'. He's not drivin' the Infiniti. He's got a Toyota rental. The Infiniti is probably still in Mexico getting fixed up to cover up the damage. He's with some friends. We figure when they've done some more drinkin', they'll come staggering out. Then we drag Basil Bustos into the alley and get the truth out of him."

Paul was talking so loudly that Luis Sandoval heard the gist of the conversation. He pulled the car over to the shoulder of the road. Before Ernesto could answer Paul, Mr. Sandoval snatched the cell phone from

Ernesto's hand. "Paul," he said sternly, "this is Luis Sandoval, Ernie's father. Listen to me and listen good. You guys grab that guy and rough him up, and you've committed felony assault. This isn't some gangbanger you're tangling with. This is a well respected teacher's son, a rich guy's son. Basil Bustos has not been arrested and charged with anything yet. I agree with you that this guy probably caused the accident, but evidence has to be gathered. He needs to be arrested. It has to be done legally, Paul."

"Mr. Sandoval," Paul replied with exaggerated politeness. "With all due respect, this punk is gonna reclaim the Infiniti lookin' nothing like the car that almost killed Abel's father. All those slimy lawyers who got him off before will surface again. That creep is gonna walk. It ain't happening, sir."

"Paul, you're one of Ernie's best friends, and he cares about you. I care about you too, and I care about those other guys, Cruz and Beto." Luis Sandoval was working hard

191

to stop Paul from doing something rash. "I got them in school at the community college, and pretty soon they'll be making good union pay. They have a bright future. All I'm asking, Paul, is don't do anything until we get over there, okay? I don't want you guys to end up being Basil Bustos's victims too."

"Okay, that's a deal. We'll wait for you, Mr. Sandoval," Paul agreed. "But don't take too long."

Ernesto took the wheel of the minivan while his father got on the phone with his friend, Officer Jerry Davis. "Jerry, this is Luis Sandoval. You need to get a cruiser over to the Cat's Paw, that dive on Polk Street." Mr. Sandoval was speaking rapidly. "There's a young man in there drinking. His name is Basil Bustos. We're pretty sure he was driving the Infiniti that cracked up all those cars on the freeway. We think the Infiniti is getting a makeover in Mexico right now."

Luis Sandoval put down the phone and looked at Ernesto. "They're on their way."

The Sandovals parked their minivan down the street from the Cat's Paw, just behind Cruz's van. Paul, Cruz, and Beto were leaning on the van in baggy trousers and hoodies. They looked for all the world like gangbangers, getting ready for a serious rumble.

"You guys," Luis Sandoval told them, "a cop friend of mine and his partner will be here in a few minutes. I think we can get this done without anybody committing a felony. Trust me, Paul, Cruz, and Beto. I'm on your side. I just want to do it the right way, okay?"

Paul glared at Mr. Sandoval but said nothing. Cruz and Beto, Ernesto thought, looked a little relieved. Perhaps they weren't as hot as Paul was about mugging Basil.

Ernesto was proud his father—he was handling the situation.

They waited for Officer Jerry Davis to arrive. He was in plainclothes and driving his personal vehicle. Paul described Basil to the police officer and where he was sitting in the bar. Mr. Sandoval reported on the conversation that he and Ernesto had had with Mr. Bustos.

The three of them—Jerry, Mr. Sandoval, and Ernesto—entered the place. Basil Bustos was sitting at the bar, obviously drunk. No doubt, he had every intention of leaving the bar soon, when he was even drunker, and driving off in the rented Toyota. Luis Sandoval and Ernesto stood back a bit while Jerry walked up to the bar where Basil sat. The policeman flashed his badge and asked his two friends, "Would you guys excuse us a minute? I need to talk to this gentleman."

The two guys melted away, and Ernesto and his father watched at a distance.

"Are you Basil Bustos?" Jerry asked.

"Yeah, whass goin' on?" Basil asked in a slurred voice.

"I need to ask you a few questions," the police officer explained.

Even though he was very drunk, Basil suddenly looked nervous.

"Why are you here, Basil?" Jerry inquired.

"Why shouldn' I be . . . be here?" Basil replied, with a hiccup.

"Your father," Jerry replied, "says he loaned you his silver Infiniti. You were supposed to be driving it to Brandeis College. But you're not doing that. Here you are sitting in a bar in the *barrio*."

"So I'm jus' sayin' goo'-by to some friends," Basil slurred. He didn't seem to be aware of how poor his speech was. "Wass the big deal?"

"Basil," Jerry stated, "can you tell me where you were—what you were doing— last Sunday afternoon?"

"I don' remember," Basil murmured. "I went to a party or something; I think. Wass the difference?"

"Can you tell me where you car is?" Jerry asked, coolly.

"'S outside," Basil replied, starting to get up from the bar stool. "I'll show ya."

The police officer stepped in front of him and put a hand up to stop him.

"Hold on, Basil," he ordered, "not the rental outside. Where's your Infiniti? Can you tell me that?"

Basil stared at the officer for a second or two, their faces only inches apart.

"'S gettin' fixed," Basil murmured.

"Where?" Jerry persisted. "Where is it getting fixed, Basil?"

"Dunno," Basil shrugged, slumping back on the stool. "My father's takin' care of it."

"Your father," the police officer countered, "says you took the Infiniti and you're driving to school in it. He doesn't know anything about the car getting fixed. And he doesn't know you're sitting in a bar."

Basil said nothing. He just stared at the police officer, who continued speaking.

"Last Sunday, you were driving over a hundred miles an hour, and you forced several vehicles into a bad accident, Basil. Someone almost got killed—"

Basil Bustos's red-rimmed eyes flared. "I didn' do nothin'," Basil stormed. "Those idiots just started crashin' into each other. I didn't do nothin' to make it happen. I'm a . . . I'm a good driver. I wasn't drunk or nothin'. They were drivin' crazy. It was their own fault what happened."

"Where's the Infiniti, Basil?" Jerry asked again. "You sideswiped a truck going on the Washington ramp, and you got some fender damage. So where did you stash the Infiniti?"

Basil was sobering up out of fear.

"I . . . I got scared when those crazy idiots started hittin' each other," Basil stammered. "I wanted to get off the freeway fast. This lousy dump truck crumpled my back fender. I knew my old man would be mad about gettin' his car creamed. I'm gettin' it fixed in Mexico. Gonna be good as new. Everything's cool, man. I got one more drink here, and then I'm on my way."

Basil reached for his drink, but Jerry grabbed the glass and slid it away from him. The officer turned his head toward the bartender.

"You know," he said sternly, "there're laws about serving drinks to someone who's very drunk. This guy's so drunk he can hardly stand. If I wasn't here, he'd be on the road in another five minutes."

The bartender looked sheepishly at the police officer.

"*I'm not drunk!*" Basil Bustos yelled.

"You almost killed a good man on Sunday," Jerry said calmly. "A man whose little finger is worth more than your entire hide."

Then Officer Jerry Davis started the arrest of Basil Bustos. "Stand up, turn around, put your hands behind your back."

Basil hesitated.

"Do it, my friend," Jerry commanded. "Or do you want to add resisting arrest to the charges?"

Basil complied. "You're being arrested for . . . ," Jerry began.

The police officer searched Basil Bustos's pockets. He had paperwork in his wallet on where the Infiniti was being repaired in Mexico.

Outside the bar, Jerry thanked Mr. Sandoval and his son. He also nodded a thank-you and flashed a thumbs-up to Paul and his friends. Then he got on his phone to call in a request for a cruiser to take Basil in for questioning and probably booking.

Ernesto and his father went over to the van where Paul and his friends were. The young men had seen Basil Bustos being taken down.

"Thank you, Paul," Mr. Sandoval said, "for the information on Basil. You did a wonderful job of getting it."

Paul looked a little uncomfortable but finally responded.

"You were right, Mr. Sandoval," Paul admitted. "I had some time to think while you were all inside the bar. You were looking for justice. I wanted vengeance. That's not the way to go."

Then Paul's cell phone rang.

Suddenly, Paul starting laughing loudly. "That's great, man, just great! I'll be right over."

Slipping his phone into his pocket, Paul reported on the conversation.

"That was Abel," he said. "He called from the hospital. He says his dad started shiftin' around in the bed and mumbling somethin'. Nobody could figure out what he was tryin' to say."

Paul shook his head and chuckled.

"Finally," he went on, "Mrs. Ruiz, she's leaning way over the bed. She's got her ear right next to his dad's lips. His dad, he's just saying somethin' over and over. Then Mrs. Ruiz stands straight up. She shakes her head at his dad and says, '*Ay! Madre de Dios!*' And Abel is all like, 'What, Mom? What did he say? Tell us!' 'That man! When he gets better, I will kill him! Scaring me like that!' And Abel, he's sayin', 'For cryin' out loud, Mom, what did he say?'"

Paul looked at everyone. Ernesto popped his eyeballs and craned his head, as if to say, "Will *you* please tell us?"

Paul chuckled again. "He said he's hungry."